CW00403464

The Stillwell Haunting

CAT KNIGHT

Disclaimer

This story is a work of fiction, any resemblance to people is purely coincidence. All places, names, events, businesses, etc. are used in a fictional manner. All characters are from the imagination of the author.

Table of Contents

PROLOGUE

The urchins hadn't done their job. That was the beginning and end of it. The children who had plagued Stillwell all his life had not had the effect he sought. They stood on the street and chanted, but they had not driven anyone out the window. Those little street rats simply hadn't been scary enough.

Stillwell didn't like what had happened. He didn't like it at all. He had come to expect certain things, certain responses to his efforts. In his estimation, people were quite predictable. He did one thing, and they responded. Their range of emotions and thought were not vast. In his estimation, they were mostly alike, vulnerable and afraid. That they didn't believe in him was their fatal flaw. Instead of dealing with him, they doubted themselves. They supposed they were having an "event" or some sort of delusion. They worked exceedingly hard to deny his existence.

He didn't need to "exist" in order to push people over the edge, push them out the window. All he needed to do was get inside their heads, their minds. That was enough. They would do the rest, cowering in fear, or running away screaming. While he would rather they jumped, destroying their minds was almost as satisfying. Reducing them to drooling idiots hiding in the corner, that brought a certain satisfaction. And he had done it every time, every time someone thought to spend the night.

Almost every time.

The two women, the ones with their devices and bedrolls, they hadn't pitched out the window. They hadn't been assigned to a corner, blathering and sobbing. They had survived—Robynne and Marian. They had come to displace Stillwell. Ha! He had sent them packing.

But he hadn't broken them.

That was disconcerting for Stillwell. He prided himself for his ability to access human terror and exploit it. Certainly, he had made inroads with the women. He sensed that, at least, one of them wanted to jump. One of them was ready to do his bidding. One of them was ready to provide entertainment for anyone in the street below. But neither one had actually gone out the window. Neither one had to be carried out, the victim of their own unchecked fear. He considered that something of a stain.

People who spent time in the confines of his bedroom, well, those people would never be the same. Robynne and Marian, the escapees, they mocked him. The women showed him how feeble he was. Two women, the weaker sex, had managed to thwart him. That left a bitter taste—if he had had the wherewithal to taste.

They were gone.

The flies had escaped the web. The spider sat brooding, wondering how it had been accomplished. Perhaps, Stillwell was losing his touch, his skill. Perhaps, the old ways needed revamping. Certainly, times had changed. The devices the women had brought were far beyond his ken. He surmised that they had something to do with him, with what he was, but he couldn't fathom what. As far as he was concerned, the devices were things to be foiled, tossed about and destroyed. They had no effect. He had turned them to his use, knowing that even simple actions pushed people toward the edge. They lost their ability to think. That always made him smile.

But Marian and Robynne.

They should have jumped.

Stillwell was certain about that. They should have held hands and smiled at each other, as they plummeted to their death. A double jump had never been achieved before. He had been looking forward to it.

Instead, he was forced to revamp his efforts. He needed new techniques, new exercises. If he was going to achieve his goal, he would have to look past his standard practices. If he was going to reinforce his hatred, he would have to design new avenues of attack. He would have to exploit every nuance of terror.

For a moment, he wondered if he was getting too old, if it was time to move on. Would he be better off abandoning his room? Had his desire for revenge been assuaged? Was he getting soft, because he had achieved what the vengeance he wanted? Had he outlived his usefulness?

That thought almost made him laugh.

Outlive.

As if he was alive in his present form. He had an existence, but he could hardly call it a life. He had been "dead" for a long time. He would stay "dead", even if he moved on. But he couldn't move on just yet. Not after losing the two women. Moving on now was impossible. He needed a success in order to quit. Champions retired on their laurels, not their failures. Because, he really didn't feel he had achieved all he could achieve. The two women had pushed his weaknesses into the light.

And he still hated.

The shame he had felt at the altar was beyond extinguishing. It had burned him when it happened, and time hadn't smothered the flames. He had never had his revenge on "her", the woman who had jilted him. She had died without knowing his wrath. Others had experienced his pain and loathing, but not "her". He had exacted a certain pain from many people, but not from "her". While he had come to some accommodation with that, he surmised that he needed one more night, one more darkness filled with the mewling and sobbing of the truly terrified. He needed one, perhaps two mortals to imitate him and pitch out the window. Yes, that was a worthy goal. One, maybe two, perhaps three, but certain no more than three. If he could achieve that, he could vanish from this world forever.

Just one.

Or two.

Perhaps three.

Certainly, that would sate his desire. He had no idea how long he would have to wait for those people. Time wasn't something he cared about. He was here, and he hungered, and he needed just one...or two...perhaps three...more flyers. That would be enough.

Just one.

Or two.

Perhaps three.

CHAPTER ONE

Robynne gripped the pint with both hands and wondered why in the world she had agreed to go back to the house and battle Stillwell again. What was she thinking? Sure, James had been persuasive, and he had offered a bonus, but the encounter with the ghost was still fresh in Robynne's mind. She and Marian had decided to let things be. They weren't looking for a rematch. Every team lost once in a while.

But James had been charming, and he offered money, which Robynne and Marian were short of. Money was, perhaps, the most persuasive thing in the universe. So, they had accepted the gig. Round two with Stillwell. But they weren't looking for a repeat. They had brainstormed the effort, and it had been Marian who came up with the idea.

"I think I have it," Marian had said.

"What do you have?" Robynne had asked.

"The solution, what else?"

"And the solution is?" Robynne asked.

"To get rid of the ghost, to get rid of Stillwell."

"Oh, why didn't I think of that, Ms. Obvious."

"Don't be snarky. I know the theory is obvious, but the process is not. Ask yourself why Stillwell is still there."

"Because he loves to haunt the place and persuade people to jump out the window?"

"Besides that. Why won't he move on? I mean, after all this time, you would expect any self-respecting ghost to move on. How much scaring does he have to do?"

"In his case, a great deal. You do remember what happened that night, don't you?"

Marian's smile faded. "No one remembers better than me. I was ready to take a flyer, as I recall."

"Then, you know that Stillwell didn't seem ready to call it a day."

"True, but why doesn't he claim his win and leave?"

"He's still a bit angry, perhaps?"

"More than a bit. I'd say he's still full of vengeance. He can't forget that he was jilted. He can't forget how the ragamuffins treated him."

"And we change that how?"

Marian beamed. "It's simple. We get him married."

"Sounds simple to me."

"That's the beauty of this plan," Marian said. "We perform the nuptials between Stillwell and a...wait for it...live woman."

Marian's grin was as wide as the Thames. She sat back, as if she had just solved the riddle of the sphinx's smile.

"Brilliant," Robynne said. "Marvellous. Where do we find this woman of refinement, who happens to have a yen for a male ghost?"

"How would I know? I came up with the idea. I would think it's your task to actually find said woman."

"Oh, right, take out an ad in the Times? Drop a short description into a Twitter feed? 'Need one pretty, impetuous female ready to spend the rest of her life with a ghost'. I'm sure that would bring in a plethora of responses."

"I don't think it would have to be forever. After they've left on their honeymoon, we perform some sort of ritual that forever bans Stillwell from returning. That doesn't sound all that difficult."

"You're proposing that Stillwell be jilted twice. Once at the altar in real life, and once on his ghostly honeymoon. That should placate the man."

"Ghost."

"Manly ghost."

Marian frowned. "I had hoped for a better response to the idea."

Robynne had thought about it a moment before she set down her cup.

"Marian, I think you might have something."

Marian smiled. "You really think so?"

"Indeed, I do, indeed I do. But not a marriage, as Stillwell doesn't strike me as a man to be fooled twice."

"Then, what?"

"A relationship, to be sure, someone who might convince him that there's a better existence waiting."

"That someone would be?"

"How do you feel about wiccans?"

"Wiccans? You think a wiccan can tempt him?"

"I think wiccans are the only women who believe enough to even try. What do you think?"

***

Robynne replayed that scene in her mind. At the time, it seemed like a plausible plan, but now, under the bright scrutiny of a pint, it seemed bonkers. Yet, there were only two things wrong with it—Stillwell and the wiccan. It didn't seem like much could go wrong there.

Glancing at the door, she wondered when Marian would arrive. Marian had called to say she had found the perfect woman for the ghost. Well, the perfect wiccan, perhaps.

That was Marian's mission, to find a wiccan who would seduce the ghost and get it out of the house. Robynne was of the opinion that the perfect wiccan existed. Would she and Marian be able to find that ideal woman? Robynne hoped so. Her savings hoped so.

She liked what she was doing with Marian. She didn't want to give that up for a job in real estate, which was her fallback position. She didn't see herself trying to qualify ne'er-do-wells for thirty-year loans.

Robynne finished the pint as Marian entered the pub. With Marian was a woman Robynne didn't know. Marian led the woman through the mostly empty pub. They stopped at the booth.

"Robynne," Marian said. "I want you to meet Rococo."

"Hello," Robynne said. "Please take a seat."

"Rococo is interested in our…situation," Marian said, as she and Rococo sat opposite Robynne.

"I am, I am," Rococo said. "I can't wait to meet your ghost."

Robynne regarded Rococo, who didn't look like a wiccan, not in Robynne's estimation. Robynne expected someone dressed in black, perhaps with a hood. She expected long, black nails and long, black hair, and eyes rimmed in black makeup. She expected black lipstick and maybe a black heart.

That Rococo possessed short, blonde hair, red nails and lips, and brown eyes, seemed almost wrong to Robynne. Rococo also wore jeans, funky boots, and a sweatshirt that said BELIEVE IN MAGIC.

"You do know what we're asking you to do, right?"

"I do, and I'm very excited about it. While I have met several ghosts, well, not so much met, as encountered. Ghosts, in my experience, don't just open up to people. For the most part, they hide. Some seem quite shy. I ran into one that had managed to trap herself in a wishing well. Can you imagine sitting at the bottom of a well, watching the coins bounce all around you? No wonder, she was frightened."

Robynne smiled, despite the fact that she was less than impressed by Rococo, the saviour of wishing-well ghosts. But then, Robynne didn't have to like Rococo. Robynne only had to convince Rococo to meet Stillwell and lure the angry ghost out of the house for a possible relationship. Seemed reasonable on paper, but under the harsh light of the pub, the idea seemed bonkers. How had Robynne been talked into this?

"Look," Robynne said. "What we know about this Stillwell is not encouraging. We think he wants the relationship he didn't get the first time around.

Well, we hope he wants it."

"I do too," Rococo said. "I think we have the opportunity to make history. I get the chance to have a real-life relationship with a ghost. Isn't that exciting?"

"I think Robynne is trying to point out some realistic expectations," Marian said. "We want him out of the house. That's all. After that, you will have to rid yourself of him, as we don't think he's a stable ghost. That didn't come out right. But I don't think you should plan on keeping him."

"I understand your concern," Rococo said. "But I know what I'm doing. I am equipped with spells that can control ghosts. Ancient spells that have proven useful over centuries. So, I appreciate your care. But I will be able to handle this Stillwell. I've been training for him all my life."

"That is good to hear," Marian said. "But you need to know that what we're planning might be dangerous."

"No, no, no," Rococo said. "It won't be dangerous. This ghost simply needs a nudge, a reason to move out of what is clearly a very painful situation. That's how I'll do it. Persuasion. I'm very good at persuasion."

"I'm sure you are," Robynne said. "You'll get your chance to show us. How about a pint?"

"Of course," Rococo said. "I'm a Wiccan, not a nun."

Robynne laughed, as did Marian. It wasn't until the second pint that Robynne listed the things Rococo was supposed to bring to the house, to Stillwell's house.

By the time the third pint arrived, Rococo had left, giddy and humming some lilt Robynne did not recognise. That was when Marian smiled.

"Well, what do you think?" Marian asked.

"I think she's in for a rude awakening," Robynne said. "I don't remember Stillwell as some misunderstood ghost. And I have a healing rib to prove it."

"She is a ray of sunshine," Marian said. "Perhaps, that is exactly what Stillwell needs."

"We are sure it's Stillwell, aren't we?"

"They chanted his name."

"They also chanted about us."

Marian frowned. "You don't think it could be some other ghost, do you?"

"No, no, I don't. Stillwell is quite enough, if you ask me. But how do we bring reality to Rococo?"

"We don't. We bring Rococo to the reality."

Robynne laughed. "Yes, I suppose that is what must be done."

Robynne reached across the table and took Marian's hand.

"You know, we don't have to do this."

"Oh, but we do," Marian said. "Our reputation depends on it."

"I just wanted to make sure that you're a go."

"I'm a go. And this time, we're not going to get caught up in some fantasy."

"No, this time will be different."

Robynne looked into Marian's eyes.

"Are you frightened?"

"Bloody hell yes!"

CHAPTER TWO

James Darling met Robynne and Marian as they came through the front door. Robynne was not surprised. She noticed the strain that appeared in his face, and she guessed he was struggling against his better judgement. After all, the first effort to oust the ghost had met with disaster, almost complete disaster. Robynne still suffered from nightmares about the maw. Some nights, she even heard the urchins. Those were the really scary nights.

"I've taken the liberty of stocking the kitchen," he said. "There is food in the fridge and cutlery in the cabinets. There's a proper tea kettle and a coffee maker, should you need it. I've had an electrician check the wiring; everything is in working order. In fact, the house is in tip-top shape."

"We thank you," Robynne said. "And while appreciate your efforts, we do not intend to stay here long enough to make use of the kitchen. Well, not much use."

"There's plenty of hot water," he added. "So, you can bathe, should you wish to. I'm afraid there are no beds in any of the bedrooms, but you did say you didn't need them."

"We don't," Marian said. "If we sleep, and there's no guarantee of that, we'll use our sleeping bags."

"Well, then, I wish you the best of luck," he said. "If you do find you need something, ring me. I'll see what I can do." He forced a smile. "I do wish you luck. I won't say that my marriage hinges on your success, but my marriage hinges on your success."

They all chuckled. It was a stab at a joke, and it partially worked.

"No one wants this to go well more than we do," Robynne said.

"If the...ghost doesn't present itself?" he asked.

"That may happen," Robynne said. "But we don't think so. We detected a certain hubris in this ghost, a pride that we haven't encountered before."

"I hadn't thought of that," James said. "I suppose that ghosts took along all the flaws they had in real life."

Marian nodded, "Yes, and sometimes it seems as if they acquire more flaws."

"Or the faults they have become magnified," Robynne agreed "After all, without someone there to put on the brakes, a warped mind can go anywhere."

Robynne knew she and Marian had never really met a ghost before, but she thought the lie would play with James. She sounded as if she really knew ghosts.

He smiled. "I envy you in a way. You're going to battle the unknown and perhaps unknowable. What person wouldn't want that?"

"Maybe, we should trade," Marian said. "You fight the ghost, and we'll sip brandy at the club."

He laughed. "I do have one request. If you can arrange it, can you video what happens? I'm not asking you to broadcast it in real time, but I would like to see it."

"We'll do our best," Robynne said. "The last time, our cameras didn't capture anything. I'm guessing that will be the case this time too. If we get something, we'll get it to your immediately."

"Great, great. Then, I'm off. Remember, the Bobbies are only a phone call away, should you need them."

"I don't think Bobbies will be of much use against the ghost. Rest assured, however, that we will use them if we can."

As James walked out the door, Marian turned to Robynne.

"Where would you like to begin?"

"Tea," Marian said. "I would like a cup of tea. Then, the cameras. As you said, they will probably go for naught, but they might give us a bit of warning, don't you think?"

"If you attach them to the router. We'll make it so that if they go offline, we'll be notified."

"Do you have the feeling that we're heading into Dante's Inferno?"

"'Abandon every hope, all ye who enter here.'?"

"Exactly."

"Hope beats in every human heart. So, we'll always have hope, Marian. We'll win this one. Why? Because we can't afford to lose."

The tea hour passed far too quickly for Robynne. She hardly felt ready to take on the ghost that she assumed waited. While she hadn't heard any *"Jump"* yet, she could feel a certain malevolence in the air, a certain hatred. That sounded silly, even to her own ears, but it was true. If a house could possess some sort of hate, this was the house.

"Do you feel it?" Robynne asked as she rinsed teacups.

"Oh, yes," Marian answered. "It's cold, and it wants to harm us. That's what I get."

"I think we should try to stay together as much as possible."

"Because that worked so well last time?"

Robynne chuckled. "No, because numbers matter. We stand a much better chance together than separated."

"Two heads are better than one. Well, two clear heads are better than one."

"When is Rococo due?"

Marian glanced at her watch. "Another hour or so. That's one of the irritating things about Wiccans. They don't seem particularly enthused about promptness."

"Time is some sort of human construct that can be ignored. Didn't you learn that?"

"If you were talking about age, I'd be right there with you. Although trying to ignore aging doesn't seem to be working for me."

"Time is a cruel task master. So, let's get set up. Then, we can take another tea break and wait for Rococo."

True to Robynne's idea, they did not split up to perform their tasks. Marian helped Robynne with the hot spot, master router, and remote routers. Robynne helped Marian with the cameras, making sure they all worked and were connected to the router network. She was certain that should a camera fail, they would be immediately notified.

A failure would be some sort of early warning system, because Robynne wanted to be forewarned, in the event the ghost acted.

After the devices had been deployed, Robynne and Marian returned to the kitchen. The tea tasted better than ever. Since they had brought some biscuits with them, they had a regular snack.

"Do you ever think that maybe you imagined everything that happened last time?" Marian asked.

"I didn't imagine a cracked rib."

"Oh, I know the physical hurts couldn't be hallucinations, but the chants and the words, the floor. Do you think those were all inside your head?"

"Some of it was. After all, the floor couldn't have really tilted, could it? But I believe most of it occurred at some level."

"In some other dimension?"

"Possibly. If the ghost exists in another plane, why can't it bring that to us?"

"That's a cheery thought. We go from good, old safe London to horrific, unpredictable London."

"I'm not saying it will happen. I'm just saying that it could happen."

"And if it does?"

"I think we would need to hold hands," Robynne said. "The last thing we want is to be separated into two different worlds."

"You're scaring me," Marian said.

"Don't worry about it. If Rococo is half as good as she claims to be, she'll soon have a date for the Queen's Jubilee."

"Queens still have Jubilees?"

"Of course, they do. It's tradition, and you know how Brits love their traditions."

"Almost as much as they love their pints."

"By the way," Robynne said. "I did bring a bottle of whiskey...should we need it."

"I was hoping James would stock the larder with one, but yours will do nicely."

At the end of an hour, Robynne and Marian, keeping their togetherness pledge, made a round of the devices. The routers and cameras were working per specifications. So far, so good. It was as they were heading back to the kitchen that Robynne's phone pinged.

"She's on her way," Robynne said.

"We're going to overlook her name and beliefs, correct?" Marian asked.

"She can worship a three-headed monkey for all I care. If she gets Stillwell out of the house, she's aces with me."

"Amen to that."

Thirty minutes later, Rococo entered the kitchen. Her backpack was much like the others, but she didn't have a sleeping bag attached.

"No sleeping bag?" Robynne asked.

"I don't intend to be here overnight. After all, it's just a ghost. Now, if you were taking on a hobgoblin, well, that would be different."

Robynne didn't want to ask how different a hobgoblin could be. A ghost had proved difficult enough.

"Where do I set up?" Rococo asked.

Robynne and Marian, who had become twins in a way, led Rococo to the master bedroom. They stood aside as Rococo walked to the middle of the room and closed her eyes. She raised one finger, lest Robynne or Marian showed the gall to interrupt her communion with the spirits. Robynne thought it was all a rather rehearsed show, but she wasn't about to make that comment. Instead, she waited patiently, until Rococo opened her eyes.

"These cameras will have to go," Rococo said.

"Say again?" Marian asked.

"He is quite angry," Rococo said. "And these cameras are very off putting, if you get what I mean. How can he communicate with all the cameras in place?"

"He managed to last time," Robynne said. "Well, he disabled them first, so I suppose you're making sense. But we would like to establish his existence. You can understand that."

"When it's over, you will have three expert witnesses. What more do you need?"

Robynne looked at Marian.

"It's her show," Marian said. "And she's right. Who would believe a video anyway?"

Robynne and Marian removed the cameras and router. Robynne wasn't at all sure that they were doing the right thing, but she couldn't protest too much. It was Rococo's show.

Once the cameras had been stowed, Rococo went about installing her own props. She laid out thick, white candles in a circle, which prompted Marian to ask why they weren't in a pentagram. Rococo was quick to point out that they weren't after a demon. Ordinary ghosts were often fearful of pentagrams. A circle had no sharp points, and therefore was non-threatening. In fact, it would invite the ghost into their presence. The last thing they wanted to do was scare the ghost. That would defeat their purpose.

After the candles, Rococo put samovars outside the circle. The samovars formed a cross. Robynne resisted the urge to ask about the samovars, but it didn't matter. Rococo offered an explanation anyway.

"I use samovars," she said, "because I prefer scented water vapor over incense. Incense is so heavy, don't you think? It always reminds me of church, or perhaps a Turkish coffee shop."

"Sounds delightful," Marian said. "I never would have thought of it."

"You should try it sometime," Rococo said. "It's excellent for those cold, grey, November days, when you think the sun will never shine again. I recommend lilac and vanilla."

Robynne was tempted to scream. What did all the scents and candles and whatever have to do with getting the ghost out of the house? But Robynne held her passion in check. An agreement was an agreement.

After the samovars Rococo pulled out a small rug that she placed in the centre of the circle.

"Ghosts need to be anchored," Rococo explained. "The rug will be his anchor, even though he really can't sit there."

Robynne wasn't about to ask why the ghost needed to sit. She was hoping for a whirlwind affair. No courting, no kissing, no hesitation. Rococo came with a backpack and would leave with a ghost. Seemed fair to Robynne.

After she spread the rug, Rococo looked about the room. She smiled, pleased. "We're ready," she said and headed for the door.

"Where are you going?" Marian asked.

"We have to let him get used to the items," Rococo said. "Which gives us time for a spot of tea."

"Do you really want to leave your things around an angry ghost?" Robynne asked.

"He is intimately familiar with everything, there is no reason for him to feel threatened." Rococo seemed sure in her judgment.

"We did tell you he's not exactly kind," Marian replied

"He did try to chuck us out the window," Robynne added.

"A misunderstanding, I'm certain," Rococo shrugged her shoulders. "Come along. Some herbal tea, a sugar-free biscuit, we'll all feel better."

At that moment, a blast of cold air slammed into them. It was something from the Antarctic.

"Oh my," Rococo visibly shivered. "That is a tad unfriendly."

Robynne wanted to tell Rococo that the icy air was nothing compared to what the ghost could do. But Rococo was already gone, as if the blast meant nothing at all.

"She'll grow on you," Marian said, as they went down to the kitchen.

"So will moss," Robynne said. "I don't fancy moss either."

Behind them, the bedroom door slammed shut with a loud WHAP.

CHAPTER THREE

Robynne found Rococo more than a bit talkative, as they sipped tea in the kitchen. It seemed Rococo wanted to talk about everything but what was going to happen. Robynne found Rococo's nonchalance almost unnerving. Obviously, Rococo had never crossed paths with a particularly angry ghost. To Rococo, everything was unicorns and fairies. That attitude drove Robynne to distraction. The day was passing, and with that went the light. Robynne had no particular desire to try Stillwell in the dark.

"I suppose we should get on with it," Marian said, with slight reluctance.

"You're right," Rococo agreed. "I've put it off long enough. Let's fetch this ghost—"

"Stillwell," Robynne interjected.

"This Stillwell ghost," Rococo said. "And tempt him out the door."

As they ascended the stairs, Robynne felt no resistance. She had expected a blast of cold air or some sort of barrier. But there was nothing. For a moment, she wondered if Stillwell had already abandoned the house. No, she knew better. It was more like some sort of plant that lured in unsuspecting insects and devoured them.

The lights worked, and Robynne was happy for the light. She watched as Rococo went about lighting the candles. To Robynne, the candles were lit willy-nilly, without any discernible pattern. Was that correct? Was there supposed to be some sort of ritual? Certainly, it made a difference if the candles were lit left-to-right or right-to-left, didn't it?

"Now," Rococo said. "I'm thrilled to be doing this. So, if you'll turn off the lights, we can call forth our friend."

"He's not our friend," Marian quipped. "I wish you would remember that."

"Shhhh," Rococo put a finger to her lips and then continued on flamboyantly. "Of course, Stillwell is our friend. That is why we are offering him a way to forsake this rather shabby existence and move to a higher plane—with me."

Robynne killed the lights as requested and stood back from the circle. The drapes were closed, which made the room dark. Not as dark as night, but dark enough. Black shadows occupied the corners, like sentinels ready to pounce.

"Stillwell," Rococo said loudly. "We are here to offer you a chance to leave with honour and respect. My name is Rococo. I will be your friend and your guide. I will be the companion you have always wanted. I will fill that empty space in your heart. We will be more than friends. We will be of one heart and mind. Come forth and greet me."

Nothing happened, and Robynne remained thoroughly unimpressed. She glanced at Marian, who rolled her eyes. The opening was not something to be lauded.

"Stillwell," Rococo said. "I want to do this amicably. We are not here to hurt you. We are here to help. We are here so that you can fulfil your destiny."

Snicker.

The snicker was low and wide and filled the room. Robynne felt her body tense. She looked about, wondering what was coming. She noticed Marian had backed against a wall, not allowing anything to get behind her. Robynne followed suite. The firmness of the wall felt amazingly good.

"Now, now," Rococo said. "This is a legitimate offer. We want to help. We want you to find peace and love."

Laugh.

Robynne shivered. The laugh was ten times worse than the snicker. It was filled with contempt and loathing, snarky with contempt.

31

Rococo filled the room with a singsong bit of something. Robynne had no idea what it was.

"Made of Nothing,

"Made of all.

"Made of summer.

"Made of fall.

"Made of winter.

"Made of spring.

"Made of silence.

"Made of sing."

Robynne frowned, as the rhyme meant nothing. She had the feeling that is was just some drivel Rococo had made up for the occasion.

"Made of thought.

"Made of feel.

"Made of wishes

"To be real"

Rococo tossed what appeared to be sparkling, silver stars into the air. In the flickering light, they glittered like the real thing.

Robynne froze.

The glittering stars floated for a moment, before they took on a shape, a form, and the shape was that of a man. There could be no doubt about that.

A man made of glittering stars appeared in front of them. He stood exactly on the rug Rococo had laid down. Wonder joined the fear Robynne felt. What in bloody hell had Rococo done?

"Isn't that better?" Rococo said. "Don't you feel alive again? This is as you should be, Stillwell. This is the friend I wish to have."

As Robynne watched, the starry figure moved, slowly, one hesitant step at a time. It was as if he had recovered from a severe injury that limited his mobility. A man learning to walk for the second time.

"That's it," Rococo said. "You are learning what it means to trust. We are here to help. You can have faith in us. I will be with you from now on. You can find joy."

The figure slowly edged out of the circle. It stopped a foot away from Rococo, who smiled with genuine happiness. Robynne was stunned, too amazed to move or speak. In fact, she was pretty sure that speaking would damage the spell and ruin what Rococo had achieved.

Rococo held out her arms.

Stillwell (Robynne was certain it was Stillwell) slowly raised his starred arms. Robynne felt she was witnessing the meeting of two lovers. It was something from a movie.

"You are loved," Rococo said. "Accept and come with me."

Happiness flowed through Robynne. She wondered how she had assumed this would go badly. She smiled, knowing that Rococo was doing things Robynne and Marian could only dream of. Robynne was certain that Rococo and Stillwell would trade a kiss. It was perhaps the most romantic thing Robynne had ever seen.

Then, Stillwell's hand found Rococo's cheek. It looked to be a lover's caress, gentle fingers running down soft skin. Rococo didn't flinch. She smiled, letting Stillwell feel for the first time in decades. No novel or movie could hope to match the sheer loveliness of the gesture.

Woman and star-man.

In the flicker of candles.

Something for the ages.

Stillwell's other hand found Rococo's other cheek. Tears formed in Robynne's eyes. She felt her heart yearn. This was...perfect.

Stillwell's hands moved faster than Robynne could imagine.

In an instant, the star hands wrapped around Rococo's neck. She YELPED with fear and pain.

For some moments, Robynne did nothing, too surprised to move. She stared as Rococo reached up to grab the star-arms, and her fingers disrupted the glittering stars for a moment, but only for a moment.

It was as if she were trying to grab fog. Even though she had disrupted the stars they quickly coalesced into arms again, into hands that were choking the life from her. Robynne was paralyzed. This was like nothing she had ever seen in her life.

LAUGH.

The sheer evil of the cackle sent a stab of ice to Robynne's heart. Pain raced through her body, and she shook violently. For some seconds, she could think of nothing but trying to get warm. This was the most horrible feeling she had ever experienced. Her heart felt frozen, as cold as dark side of the moon.

A gasp escaped her lips, and Robynne felt her heart pound in one huge beat. It was as if her chest had become some sort of pump, shooting hot life through her veins. In an instant, she had pushed off the wall, heading for Rococo and Stillwell. Rococo's gagging was growing weaker. Robynne felt the need for speed.

The candles winked out.

The sudden dark slowed Robynne. She could still make out the figures, but Stillwell no longer glittered like ice. Rococo had become just a black shape. Something inside Robynne told her to stop, to not come in contact with the spectre. She needed to just stop and watch.

She couldn't do that.

She charged right through Stillwell.

Robynne expected some sort of collision, a crash, but she passed right through the stars, as if they were nothing but a swarm of insects. She felt them, but they didn't stop her. In an instant, she was through and turning. Even as she did, the stars realigned themselves, and Stillwell continued the choking. It was the eeriest thing she had ever seen, something to behold, if she had had time. There was no time.

She charged again.

Right through the stars.

Showing no effect, as the small things glommed back together. Robynne didn't look at Rococo. Robynne didn't want to see the anguish. Then, even as Robynne watched, Marian ran straight through Stillwell. Again, the small stars were sent hither and yon, but they immediately reformed. The attack continued, as if Marian had done nothing.

LAUGH.

LAUGH.

It was all Robynne could to hold herself together.

"Together," Robynne said.

Holding hands, Robynne and Marian ran through Stillwell together. This time, the stars flitted about the room like so many fireflies.

But as Robynne turned, she noticed that the stars were racing back to form Stillwell, to form the creature that was killing Rococo.

"What now?" Marian asked.

Robynne didn't have an immediate answer. She knew that the charging would do little good. Yet, what else was there? She panted and stared, now certain that Rococo was soon to die.

"We take his space," Robynne said.

"What?"

"Come on." Robynne grabbed Marian's hand. "Don't let go."

Robynne pulled Marian into Stillwell, and this time, they simply stood inside him, taking up the space where he stood.

What happened next was terrifying, as the stars danced about, trying to reform Stillwell. But with Robynne and Marian in the way, the stars could do little but bump into them and bounce off, seeking a way to become alive again. It felt as if a horde of flies were trying to pass through Robynne. She closed her eyes and held Marian's hand and withstood the stars that transformed from small flies to pointed darts. With a speed Robynne thought impossible, the stars hit her face and arms and hands, stinging like so many small bees.

She wondered if they were drawing blood, but she knew better than to check. Opening her eyes would allow them to blind her. They had already filled her ears.

"HANG ON!" Robynne called out.

"I AM." Marian answered.

Moments later, the stinging stopped. Robynne heard Rococo collapse, hitting the floor with a thud. Still, she didn't let go of Marian's hand. There was safety in their grip.

"Is it over?" Marian whispered."

"I'm going to open my eyes," Robynne answered.

Robynne opened her eyes. In the darkness, she could see the glittery stars all about, lifeless on the floor.

"It's stopped," Robynne said and released Marian's hand.

In an instant, Robynne was on the floor, kneeling beside Rococo, searching for a pulse.

"Is she…" Marian asked.

In Rococo's neck, Robynne found a faint pulse.

"She's not dead," Robynne said. "Turn on the lights."

Robynne rubbed Rococo's hands. The lights came on, and Robynne spotted stars embedded in Rococo's neck. The stars formed the shape of fingers, fingers that had tried to throttle her.

"What the bloody hell," Robynne said.

"What?" Marian asked.

"He tried to strangle her."

"Oh, my god," Marian said. "That's wicked."

"Should we move her?" Robynne asked.

"No," Marian said. "Not yet. Let's get her awake."

Robynne continued to rub Rococo's hand. "Wake up," Robynne pleaded "Wake up. I want to hear your voice. Come on, now, you know you want to wake up."

Robynne thought she detected a bit more colour in Rococo's cheeks, but Robynne couldn't be sure. The light wasn't that good. Yet, Robynne was more than a bit thankful for the light. The starry attack had unnerved Robynne. She was hoping for a dram of whiskey, something hot that would melt away the ice that was still attached to her heart. She had sometimes wondered why people sipped whiskey on winter days. Now, she knew. They needed something to keep the hideous cold at bay.

Rococo moaned.

Robynne smiled. "That's right," she said. "That's good. Wake up, now. Wake up, so we can share a cuppa."

Rococo's eyes opened.

Robynne had never seen such frightened eyes in her life.

The lights went out.

LAUGH

CHAPTER FOUR

Rococo moaned, as Marian came into the room.

"Don't panic," Robynne said.

"What?" Marian asked.

"Don't panic," Robynne said louder, remembering that their ears were filled with plastic stars. "Let's get her up."

They managed to get Rococo to her feet. She stood unsteadily between them.

"We're going to go down to the kitchen," Robynne told Rococo. "Are you ready?"

Rococo nodded.

"Don't let go of her," Robynne told Marian.

The window behind them opened.

Robynne felt it. She felt the maw behind her, the hungry window, she heard the urchins.

STILLWELL WENT TO WED

ON A LOVELY SUMMER DAY.

HE STOOD ALONE AT THE ALTAR

TILL THE PASTOR WENT AWAY.

WHY WAS HE THE LAST TO KNOW

THAT SHE HAD FOUND ANOTHER BEAU?

"What's that?" Rococo asked, her voice trembly.

"Never mind," Marian said. "Let's go...now!"

They started for the door. Robynne hoped they would make it. She waited for the floor to tilt, to push them toward the open window. She sensed how confused and scared Rococo was. Robynne had been through it before. She fought the fear rising in her mind. Rococo hadn't had the experience. Robynne hoped things wouldn't get any worse. But the floor remained flat, and they were able to slip out of the room. In a minute, they were in the kitchen. Robynne went to make the tea. Marian sat by Rococo at the table.

"How are you feeling?" Marian asked.

"I...I really am not sure," Rococo answered. "That wasn't the encounter I was expecting."

"He did appear," Robynne said.

"Indeed, he did, and, for a moment, all was well," Rococo said. "In a way, it was quite pretty."

"Before he strangled you," Marian said.

"Oh, that," Rococo said. "I think we set him off. He fought back because we threatened him."

Robynne looked at Rococo, and where Robynne expected to see a woman in tears, or at least in shock, Rococo seemed totally nonplussed. It was as if nothing had happened. That was as strange as Stillwell himself. Robynne added a bit of whiskey before she served the tea, which brought a smile to Rococo's face.

"The wonders of tea are so often overlooked," Rococo said. "Was the window that he opened the same as last time?"

"It is," Marian answered. "We assumed it was the window he pitched out of."

"And the children?"

"We believe they were present when his death occurred. They are rather nasty children."

"Indeed, but then, children have to be tamed. They don't become useful citizens overnight."

They sat at the table, sipping tea and eating biscuits, pulling little silver stars from their ears. Robynne wanted to ask, but she couldn't bring herself to question Rococo. What would they be able to do once Rococo left? "I know what you're thinking," Rococo said.

"You're wondering when I'll use the good sense I was born with and leave. Well, I see this as a once-in-a-lifetime opportunity. I have never experienced anything like this. I would like to take another go at Stillwell."

"You're kidding," Marian said. "He attacked you. He choked you. He wants to pitch you out the window."

"He didn't choke me to death, and I didn't go out the window, and there are three of us. That should be more than enough to handle him. I must remember not to use stars or something else he can put against us."

"What are you talking about?" Robynne said. "You're not thinking of going back up there, are you?"

"Why not?" Rococo said and rubbed her neck. "Oh, I admit I was on the losing side before. But that was because he caught me totally by surprise. He didn't seem at all angry or dangerous before. So, I let him get close."

"If you're going to entice him out of the house, you'll have to get him close," Marian said.

"I'm not so sure," Rococo said. "I think that if I do it a bit differently, I'll get him out. But, the first thing we have to do is close that window."

"Why?" Robynne asked.

"The window and the children provide the psychic energy he needs to do what he does. Without the window and the chanters, he will be easier to deal with."

"You're kidding," Robynne said.

"No, you were there. You heard the children. They bring a lot of power."

"No," Robynne said. "You don't really want to go back up there, do you?"

"I don't see how we can avoid it," Rococo said.

"But he tried to kill you," Marian's voice had the slightest hint of hysteria.

"He tried to kill you too, didn't he?" Rococo asked. "I mean, I don't think that should deter us."

Robynne looked at Marian, who raised her eyebrows.

"I suppose she's right," Marian sighed. "If closing the window will help, I'm all for it. But how do we rid ourselves of the children?"

"I think they will vanish when the window is closed. After all, their contribution to his death came because of the open window, correct?"

"We think so," Robynne nodded. "Do you want to go home and sleep on this?"

"I should hope not," Rococo answered. "If I start to think on it, I might not do it at all."

"That sounds like a pretty good strategy," Marian responded.

Rococo pulled her hand away from her coffee mug and held it up. The trembling was noticeable.

"See?" Rococo said. "It's not as if I'm not scared. I would be a fool not to be. But I have the chance to do something incredible. I have been a wiccan for some years, and I have never been so close to a real ghost. That's something."

"All right," Robynne managed. "But you now know what it's like up there. So, if we're going back, and I'm not certain that's a good idea, we have to have some sort of plan."

"Especially for the window," Marian added.

Rococo thought a moment. "We start the same as before, candles, talk, invitation."

"Do you think he'll use the stars again?" Robynne asked.

"He might, but what he can't do is engage all of us at the same time. If he should latch onto me in some fashion, he can't stop you two from closing the window."

"We have to close the window?" Marian asked.

Rococo nodded.

"It's almost dark," Robynne said. "Should we wait till morning?"

"No," Rococo answered. "We need to get this done now. If we wait, he might retreat into some dimension where we can't reach him. He'll be able to mount raids on whoever is about."

"You make it sound like he's the enemy," Marian said.

"He is, and he isn't. I hope to persuade him, once the window is fastened shut."

Robynne had to give Rococo credit for courage. Stillwell had proven more than a bit creative and dangerous. Despite that, Rococo wanted to try one more time to get the ghost out of the house. Persuasion would be the tool of choice. But then, what else did they have?

"Wait," Robynne said. "We're going to close the window, which will silence the children. Then, we're going to persuade Stillwell to leave. What if he refuses? Do we have another arrow in the quiver?"

Rococo thought a moment. "I don't think so. I mean, the only real defence would be to permanently close the window."

"Permanently?" Marian asked.

"Brick it in?" Rococo asked.

"That would be permanent," Robynne said. "But would it work?"

"I think so."

"Is there some sort of ghost-bane?" Marian asked. "You know, there's garlic for vampires and wolf-bane for werewolves. Is there something that will keep ghosts at bay?"

Rococo shook her head. "Not that I'm aware of. It would be nice if there were some kind of spray, like there is for mosquitoes and other bugs."

Robynne considered Stillwell much more dangerous than a mosquito, so a repellent would be a godsend.

But ghost-bane didn't exist. They had to depend on the window. They had to close it and keep it closed.

"Before we go up there," Rococo said. "I need a few minutes of meditation."

"What?" Robynne asked.

"And I would like a pint," Marian said. "That's my idea of meditation."

Robynne laughed. "A pint sounds good to me. Rococo?"

"I've found that a bit of alcohol does wonders for meditation."

They all laughed, and Marian fetched the pints. Despite the levity, Robynne was sure that there would be no levity when they marched up the stairs. Stillwell was still there, with all his hatred. The window was open, a maw anxious to take each and every one of them.

The children were there with their chants. Perhaps, they would have one for Rococo, one as yet unheard.

There would be a reckoning. Robynne wasn't at all sure, it would lean in their favour.

"To success," Marian said.

They clinked bottles and sipped. The ale tasted magnificent. Robynne couldn't chase away the notion that it might be the last pint she ever tasted. She bit her lip at the thought and stared at the little stars on the table, the ones from their ears. She remembered what Star-Stillwell had looked like.

She remembered the hands around Rococo's neck. Glancing over, Robynne noted the red marks on Rococo's throat. Those weren't fake. They were reminders. He might try it with all of them. Could he kill them one at a time? Robynne gripped the bottle with both hands. Some small voice in the back of her head told her that going back to the master bedroom was a mistake. What they needed was a bricklayer, not a wiccan. As she watched, Rococo stood, took her pint, and walked out of the kitchen.

"I'm not sure about this," Marian said.

"She seems OK with it," Robynne said.

"He tried to kill her."

"He's tried to kill us."

"Not by choking."

"No, by pitching us out the window."

"We have to have some kind of limit," Marian said.

"Limit?"

"If we can't get it done in, say, fifteen minutes, we bail. The longer we stay, the more dangerous it will get."

"I agree. So, a quarter-hour sounds good to me," Robynne said. "As long as Rococo isn't making progress. If things are going well, then, we stay, all right?"

"We can't abandon her, not after what happened."

Robynne stood. "I'm going down to the library and rest. If I fall asleep, wake me."

"Trust me, no one is going up there without you."

Robynne took her pint and found a corner in the library that wasn't too uncomfortable. She leaned back and closed her eyes, promising herself that a fifteen-minute nap was all she needed. While her fingers trembled, they were not as bad as before. Crossing her arms in front of her, she sought warmth and comfort. Sleep would be a good thing.

When Robynne woke, she felt very cold. Her neck and back were stiff and achy, and she had to roll to her hands and knees before she managed to stand. The room was utterly dark, which was not what it should have been.

Frowning, she looked at her watch. Then, she shook her head and rubbed her eyes.

It couldn't be.

She pulled out her mobile and looked at it. The mobile time matched the watch. What the bloody hell. It couldn't be, but it was. It was midnight.

Where were Marian and Rococo?

Midnight.

Impossible.

Robynne headed for the stairs and the kitchen.

Midnight.

That couldn't be a good thing, not for anyone.

CHAPTER FIVE

Robynne fairly ran for the kitchen, hoping she had not missed anything important and wondering why no one had come looking for her.

"Sorry," she announced as she entered the kitchen.

No one answered.

Robynne looked around the room and found it empty. She frowned. What in bloody hell was going on?

"Sorry, I'm late." Robynne turned to the voice.

Marian yawned as she entered the room. "Why didn't you wake me?"

"Because I've just now woken up," Robynne said. "Where is Rococo?"

"Here."

Through the door walked Rococo, all smiles. "Wasn't that refreshing?"

"It's midnight," Robynne said, slightly annoyed. "It's dark. We were going to take a fifteen-minute break."

"I know, apparently Stillwell didn't want us to come back right away. So, we have to do it on his terms."

"I'm not so sure I want to do it on his terms," Marian said.

"I'm afraid that makes no difference," Rococo replied.

"We could leave and come back tomorrow."

Rococo shook her head. "Now is the time. We have the advantage."

"How in bloody hell do you think that?" Robynne asked.

"We know where he is and how to affect him. We close the window and then convince him that he's better off somewhere else."

"It sounds so simple," Marian said.

"It is. Shall we?"

Robynne handed out torches. "I'm guessing the lights won't work, and the candles won't stay lit. So, let's not be lost in the dark."

"While I don't think we'll need these, I will take one. Let's go."

Robynne and Marian allowed Rococo to take the lead. She marched up the steps, humming some song Robynne didn't recognize.

Marian whispered to Robynne, "She's bloody chipper."

"She thinks this will be a lark."

"Let's be ready to abandon ship."

"Let's make sure she comes with."

The door to the bedroom was closed. Rococo was the first to reach it, and it wouldn't open.

"Stuck," Marian said.

Rococo pulled at the door. "More likely held in place by him."

"I'll try," Robynne offered. She turned the knob and pushed, and the door opened, as if on oiled hinges.

"He must like you," Rococo said. "Come on, let's be quick about setting up."

Once inside, they discovered that the lights did work, which allowed them to reset the scattered candles quickly. Even as one was set, Rococo was there to light it. Soon, the wavering light of candles joined the electric lights. It was only then that Robynne looked over that window, the open window that was nothing but a black hole, an abyss. As she stared, the darkness seemed to pulse, a slight expansion and contraction, like some kind of heart, a totally black heart. She looked away, as a cold spasm raced up her spine.

"Lights," Rococo said.

Marian turned off the lights, leaving them in the macabre candlelight.

"Stillwell," Rococo said loudly. "We have returned as friends. We wish to offer you a way out of this confinement. Let us reason together. Come forth and greet us."

Nothing happened. Robynne looked about, but her eyes always returned to the window, the beating, ebony heart.

"Stillwell," Rococo said. "We are not here to hurt you. We take no umbrage over what happened earlier. You are frightened. We understand. We are here to help. We are here so that you can fulfil your destiny."

Chuckle.

The chuckle made Robynne ball her hands into fists. She tore her eyes away from the window.

"Now, now," Rococo said. "This is a legitimate offer. We want you to find peace and love."

Rococo filled the room with a singsong bit of something. Robynne had no idea what it was.

"Made of Nothing,

"Made of all.

"Made of summer.

"Made of fall.

"Made of winter.

"Made of spring.

"Made of silence.

"Made of sing."

"Made of thought.

"Made of feel.

"Made of wishes

"To be real"

Rococo didn't throw anything this time. She merely waited. Robynne's eyes once again drifted to the window. She wondered what made the dark throb. She had the notion that if she touched the blackness, it would feel warm and inviting, like a dog or cat. That was what she was searching for. The darkness was like a pet. She could stroke it and feel it and find companionship with it.

In fact, she was certain that the darkness was the perfect pet, one that needed no real care. No feeding, no walking, no beds or rugs or cages, nothing but her gentle touch. It was already trained; she was certain of that. It wouldn't howl at the moon or bark in the middle of the night. It would be with her wherever she went, the thing she most loved and needed. She was sure that it would listen to her secrets and never mock her, the perfect friend. Always there when she needed it, always faithful. Who could ask for more?

No one.

Robynne was ready to claim her pet, when Rococo spoke.

"We'll have to close it," she said.

For a moment, Robynne wondered what Rococo was talking about. Then, she remembered. They were to close the window. But they couldn't close the window, not on her newfound pet. Perhaps, she could entice it into the room. Then, they might close the window.

"Let's do it," Marian said.

"Wait," Robynne said. "Are you sure we have to?"

"We talked about this," Marian said. "The window has to go."

"But it's out there."

"What's out there?"

Robynne was at a loss for words. She didn't know how to describe the wonderful thing that waited for her.

"The dark," Robynne said. "The dark is out there."

"We can see that," Marian said. "So?"

"You don't understand," Robynne said. "It's not the dark, it's the *dark*. Don't you see? It's there for us. It's alive."

"Alive?" Marian asked. "Are you all right?"

"I'm fine," Robynne smiled. "I'm better than fine. It wants us to love it."

"Stop," Rococo said. "Robynne, look at me."

Robynne turned reluctantly and found Rococo smiling.

"Don't look at the window," Rococo said. "Not yet."

"But it wants us."

"Of course, it does. But it's not the window that wants you. It's Stillwell. He's the one that calls you like some kind of ancient siren."

"You're wrong. It's not like that."

"It's exactly like that."

Robynne started to turn her head.

"Don't look," Rococo commanded and grabbed Robynne's arms. "Look at me."

Robynne frowned, feeling some grave injustice had been levelled on her. The dark, the wonderful dark beckoned, and she needed to go to it. This woman, this wiccan, this interloper was stopping Robynne from getting what was hers. That wasn't proper. It wasn't fair, not fair at all.

"Help me," Rococo said to Marian.

Robynne felt Marian grab one arm.

"What are you doing?" Robynne demanded. "It's warm and loving. I have to go to it."

"It is the grave," Rococo said. "While the grave can tempt, it cannot fulfil. Close your eyes. Breathe."

Robynne closed her eyes, and she immediately felt different. There was an urgent need to open them and look at the window, but the longer she kept her eyes closed, the less urgent the desire became.

Why had she needed to look at the window? To look at the dark? Had she actually thought to go pet it, like some kind of panting dog? Had she thought to be FRIENDS with it? How bonkers was that? One didn't embrace the dark. One didn't step out a window to own it.

"Keep them closed for a few more seconds," Rococo said. "Until the need goes away."

"Shit," Marian said.

"What is it?" Robynne asked, her eyes still closed.

"The lights," Marian said.

"And the candles?"

"Still lit for the moment."

"Stillwell is not coming," Rococo said. "So, we must move on. We must close the window."

"Are you certain we can?" Marian asked.

"I think so," Rococo said. "But it won't be easy."

Feeling no need to find the dark, Robynne opened her eyes. She was faced away from the window, from the dark, but she no longer felt the desire to embrace it.

"All better?" Rococo asked.

"I think so," Robynne asked. "That was...strange."

"I think we had best be at it," Rococo said.

A cold blast hit them.

"Bloody hell," Marian said. "I'm about to freeze."

"Come on," Robynne said and faced the window. "Let's do it."

Before they took a step, the candles blew out. That didn't stop them, as they turned on their torches. Even as the urchins began to chant.

STILLWELL WENT TO WED

ON A LOVELY SUMMER DAY.

HE STOOD ALONE AT THE ALTAR

TILL THE PASTOR WENT AWAY.

WHY WAS HE THE LAST TO KNOW

THAT SHE HAD FOUND ANOTHER BEAU?

"Don't stop," Rococo said.

"Bloody paupers," Marian said.

MARIAN WENT TO BED

ON A LOVELY SUMMER NIGHT,

HER EYES WERE CLOSED TO ALL.

AND SHE DIDN'T OPEN THEM

UNTIL SHE STARTED TO FALL

Even as they took another step, the floor tilted up, suddenly becoming very steep.

"Hold hands," Rococo said.

They grabbed hands and struggled, their torches flicking in every which way.

SHE-ROBYNNE SAT ON THE SILL,

CONSIDERING HER PLIGHT.

WITH FIRM RESOLVE,

SHE SOUGHT TO SOLVE

ERE SHE TOOK TO FLIGHT.

"She-Robynne is you?" Rococo asked.

"They're inventive."

"And powerful."

POOR ROCOCO IS A WITCH

WHOSE MAGIC NEVER WORKED.

SHE FOUND HERSELF OUTSIDE THE ROOM

AND FLYING WITHOUT A BROOM

"Oh my," Rococo said. "They are wicked, aren't they."

Robynne looked up and was scared. Despite their efforts, they appeared no closer to the window. She could swear they had taken steps, more than a few steps, and while it was uphill, they should be closer.

"We're not making progress," Robynne said.

LAUGH

The laugh was mean and nasty, and for a moment, Robynne found her will ebbing.

"I hate that," Marian said.

"It's evil," Rococo said.

"Don't stop," Robynne said.

Still holding hands, torches on, they plodded, the window still as far away as ever. Robynne didn't know if the window was getting no closer or their brains were being manipulated. One thing she was thankful for was that the blackness no longer throbbed, no longer spoke to her. It was just the night.

"I have to stop," Marian said. "I can't breathe."

They paused, and Marian panted.

"How are you?" Robynne asked Rococo.

"I have a raging headache," Rococo said. "But I'm not sure it's real, if that makes sense."

"It does. This is like climbing a mountain," Robynne said.

"Are you afraid?"

"Bloody hell yes," Robynne answered.

"All right," Marian said. "Let's do it."

They started again, even as the urchins chanted. Their voices filled the room, blasting into Robynne's ears. It was as if she were standing right next to them, as they shouted their inanities. She looked up. The window was closer now. A sense of urgency grabbed her. She had the idea that they needed to be quick about what they were doing. Stillwell might not yet know their intention. When he figured it out, he would find all manner of ways to thwart them.

"I'm soooo cold," Marian said.

Robynne didn't feel the cold. She leaned into the slope and pushed, willing herself to keep moving. The window was but a few steps away now, up the tilt. She wasn't yet sure what they would do when they reached the window. Since it was wide open, she wondered what had happened to the glass and wood. Not that it mattered.

"Just a bit more," Robynne said.

"I don't know if I can make it," Marian said.

It was at that moment that a thick, round candle slammed into Marian's head, and she staggered. Coming from the dark, the candle hadn't been seen.

"Marian!" Robynne said.

She was too late. A second candle hammered Marian, and she dropped to the floor. Robynne dropped to her knees and shined her torch on Marian, even as Robynne cursed Rococo for bringing the candles in the first place.

Then, a candle slammed into Rococo's neck, and she YELPED.

Robynne turned and saw the candle that hit Rococo rolling along the floor, disappearing into the darkness.

"Oh god," Rococo said as another candle just missed her face.

"Get down," Robynne said. "Get down."

Before Rococo could get down, the floor tilted again, this time toward the window.

Rococo SCREAMED.

Robynne heard the candle THUNK against Rococo's head. Robynne looked up, to see Rococo staggering along the tilting floor, heading straight for the...

Maw.

CHAPTER SIX

Robynne did the only thing she could think to do. She grabbed Rococo's arm and tried to stop the hurtling body. But Rococo's momentum was too much. Robynne could do nothing but hang on as the wiccan pitched out the window. There was a moment when Robynne thought she would lose her grip. Instead, she suddenly worried that she would be pulled out the window by Rococo, whose SCREAM filled the room.

For Robynne, the work consisted of bracing herself against the wall, to keep from tipping out the window. At the other end of her arms, Rococo was twisting and kicking and fighting. Robynne knew that she would never be able to pull a kicking Rococo back into the room.

"STOP!" Robynne yelled. "JUST STOP!"

Rococo stopped, letting herself just hang.

"That's better," Robynne said. "Don't fight me." Robynne looked down at Marian, who seemed dazed.

"Marian!" Robynne said. "Help me!"

Marian didn't respond, and Robynne wondered if Marian had been hurt in all the commotion.

"MARIAN!" Robynne barked.

Marian turned to Robynne, blinking, and Robynne knew Marian was in some kind of fugue. Robynne didn't need Marian in a fugue. Robynne needed her fully alert and strong.

"HELP ME!" Robynne ordered.

For a moment, Robynne wondered if Marian was cognizant enough to help. But then, something seemed to click. Marian stood and stared.

"Help me pull her back in," Robynne said.

Marian nodded, and she joined Robynne at the window. Robynne hadn't noticed before, but the street and other buildings had disappeared. There was only a huge black hole, over which, Rococo dangled. Robynne didn't doubt that there was concrete below them, concrete that would kill Rococo. It was only that Robynne couldn't see it. As if dropping Rococo would do no harm.

Together, Robynne and Marian pulled. Robynne's arms burned, as she had been holding on longer. Robynne could hear Rococo sobbing, hanging, not trying to help, because that would cause more problems.

"PLEASE!" Rococo sobbed. "PLEASE SAVE ME."

Robynne heard the words, but she was too busy and too fagged to answer. With Marian's help, Robynne managed to get Rococo's head and shoulders above the windowsill. Rococo grabbed what she could grab, and for the first time, Robynne thought they would save the wiccan.

"Now," Robynne told Marian. "Now, we pull hard. Once we get her hips over the sill, she'll be fine. Ready?"'

"Ready," Marian answered hoarsely.

"Now!"

Robynne strained, and Marian strained. Rococo suddenly surged back into the room, knocking down Robynne and Marian. Even as they hit the floor, they heard the urchins.

POOR ROCOCO IS A WITCH

WHOSE MAGIC NEVER WORKED.

SHE FOUND HERSELF OUTSIDE THE ROOM

AND FLYING WITHOUT A BROOM

Robynne didn't try to move. Panting, muscles on fire, she stayed on the floor, as did Rococo and Marian. For the moment, Robynne felt somewhat safe. The cold bit at her. Snarky chanting came from the urchins. She knew Stillwell wasn't far away, no doubt enjoying their pain. In a way, Robynne felt almost safe. As long as they were on the floor, they couldn't be hurt, right?

It began as a low-pitched whine. Robynne hardly noticed it, at first. As it grew louder, she wondered just what could be making the sound. She turned her head, even as Rococo covered her ears and Marian stared vacantly at the ceiling. Although Robynne didn't know what it was, she was certain it was dangerous, evil, something Stillwell had conjured up to plague them.

"We have to move," Robynne said.

She received no answers. Rococo couldn't hear, and Marian was lost for the moment.

"WE HAVE TO MOVE!" Robynne shouted.

Again, no answer from the others. Robynne's head began to ache, the sound hitting her brain over and over. She rolled up to her hands and knees and grabbed Marian's arm.

"MARIAN!" Robynne said. "MARIAN!"

Marian looked over, her eyes dull and wide.

"WE HAVE TO MOVE," Robynne said. "CAN YOU CRAWL?"

The candle slammed into Robynne's side, and she heard her rib crack. She gasped and collapsed, another candle sailing over her head. She rubbed her side, trying to rid herself of the sharp pain that came with every breath. For some seconds, she could hardly believe she had been hit. She dropped to the floor, in an effort to avoid the flying candles.

"Get down!" Robynne ordered as Marian stood. "GET DOWN!"

Robynne was too late. A candle smashed into Marian's face, and she wobbled. Then, she fell back, heading for the windowsill. Robynne grabbed Marian's leg and pulled her to the floor. Robynne heard Marian's head THUNK the floor. That couldn't be a good thing. Robynne crawled over and touched Marian's face. Blood ran out her nose.

"Marian," Robynne said, "Marian."

There was no answer. Robynne felt the back of Marian's head. There was blood there too. Concussion, was the only word Robynne could hear inside her head. What the bloody hell would she do if Marian had a concussion.

A candle missed and hit the wall. Robynne grabbed the candle and chucked it out the window. If someone in the street below got beaned, it was too bad. She couldn't allow Stillwell to have missiles to toss about.

"I have to go," Rococo said, still covering her ears. "I can't stand this."

"Crawl," Robynne said. "Don't stand. If a candle gets close, toss it out the window."

"I'm sorry about the candles," Rococo replied.

"Never mind," Robynne answered. "Get going. Get out of here."

71

Another candle hit Robynne in the shoulder, bringing instant pain. She grabbed the offending candle and pitched it. The pains shooting through her chest and shoulder and head almost overwhelmed her. The torches still gave off some shafts of light, but they were not useful, not against Stillwell.

Robynne watched Rococo crawl for the door. Then, she laid down next to Marian.

"Marian," Robynne said into Marian's ear. "We have to get out of here, but I can't do it by myself. You have to help. Do you hear me?"

Marian didn't answer. Robynne squeezed her eyes shut, fighting the whine that reverberated through her head. What was Stillwell trying to do? She kissed Marian's cheek.

"Wake up, Marian," Robynne said. "Wake up enough to help me get you out of here. Do you hear me? Stillwell is going to kill us if we stay. Do you hear? Wake up, Marian, wake up."

Marian did not respond, and for the first time, Robynne thought about leaving Marian behind. That had been unthinkable, but Robynne's rib had cracked, and her head throbbed, and she was quickly running out of energy. If she didn't leave soon, she would be stuck. Stuck with Stillwell was almost assured death. His intent was clear. He meant to kill them all. She considered a moment. Perhaps, if she left, she might be able to come back and get Marian.

That made sense. It was better for Robynne to find safe haven first. Then, she would gather others to fetch Marian. That was the sane thing to do, the safe thing to do. Trying to pull Marian out was nothing short of suicide. They would both die.

A candle slammed into Robynne's thigh, and she moaned in pain. She grabbed the offending candle and chucked it out the window. At least, she was getting rid of Stillwell's ammunition. She robbed her leg and tried to decide what to do. Because if she left Marian behind, Stillwell would pummel Marian to death. There were still enough candles left. A still body would be easy work.

Robynne looked up in time to see Rococo, torch in hand, wandering about the room. Even as Robynne looked, a candle hit Rococo in the knee, and she fell to the floor. A GROAN escaped her lips, mostly drowned out by the urchins whose chanting had grown louder. Robynne crawled over the floor, hoping to talk Rocco into helping with Marian. Robynne found an offending candle and hurled it at the window.

Missed.

She wasn't about to chase down the candle. Instead, she grabbed Rococo's hand.

"Are you all right?" Robynne asked.

"What?" Rococo asked.

"Are you all right?"

"I...I think so," Rococo answered. "We need to get out of here."

"Marian is hurt," Robynne said. "I need your help."

As Robynne watched, one of the torches jumped into the air and whipped past her, straight into the maw. She shivered, as fear raced through her brain. She had to get out. She had to get Marian out of the room. Robynne wasn't at all sure that Rococo would be able to help.

"Come on," Robynne said and grabbed Rococo's hand. "Come on."

They crawled to Marian, and Robynne was hit in the leg yet one more time. If Rococo was hit, Robynne couldn't tell.

Laugh

Robynne froze, completely unnerved by the laugh. She watched as Rococo pushed ahead, as if she hadn't heard the laugh, the awful laugh.

"Rococo," Robynne whispered. "Rococo."

Rococo didn't answer. Robynne battled the urgent feeling that she had to run, leave the others behind and just run. That was the smart thing to do. She needed to save herself. If she saved herself, she could save them. That was the best plan. Save yourself, save them.

A cold hand grabbed Robynne's neck. Icy fingers wrapped around her throat. Robynne SCREAMED and slapped at fingers she couldn't see, a hand that she couldn't touch.

"No, no, no, no, no," Robynne repeated as she pushed away the hand. Tears ran down her cheeks. She crawled ahead, seeking Rococo and Marian. Even though she no longer felt the frigid grip, she rubbed her throat, which slowed her down considerably. Yet, she managed to reach Rococo who had hold of Marian's wrist and was tugging futilely.

As Robynne watched, another candle slammed into Rococo's back, and she staggered, dropping Marian's wrist. Robynne watched as Rococo dropped to her knees, as if praying. Robynne wasn't sure of much, but she was sure that praying wouldn't help. Not here, not now.

Robynne grabbed Rococo's hand.

"You get the left hand," Robynne said. "I'll get the right. We have to pull her out. You're going to get hit by candles. Try to hide your face. If one hits you, pick it up and throw it at the window. We don't have much time. He'll keep hurting us, until he can toss us out the window. Whatever happens, keep pulling. We have to get Marian out of this room."

Robynne couldn't tell if Rococo heard or understood. Robynne hoped, because if they failed, Robynne would have to save herself.

"Now," Robynne told Rococo and stood.

To her surprise, Rococo also stood. Something had gotten through to the wiccan. Robynne leaned toward the door and pulled. Rococo did the same. They moved ten feet before a candle hit Rococo in the back. Robynne was hit in the side. Without letting go of Marian, Robynne scooped up the candle and tossed it, hoping Stillwell couldn't find it right away.

When the icy fingers brushed Robynne's cheek, she SCREECHED—but she didn't let go. Something akin to panic raced through her blood.

"Concentrate," she whispered. "Concentrate."

Tears dripped off her chin, but she hardly felt them. She stared at Marian; whose eyes were open but vacant. Robynne had the feeling Marian had suffered some kind of mind injury, something that had reduced her to a vegetable. Was it permanent? Robynne hoped not. Robynne prayed not.

"Concentrate."

A candle WHAPPED into her leg.

Rococo SCREAMED.

"KEEP GOING!" Robynne yelled.

"Concentrate."

A candle WHIZZED past Robynne's head, and she was immediately thankful.

Rococo SCREAMED.

Robynne found breathing difficult. She panted, not quite sure why she was having trouble. She looked up. The door seemed small, farther away than ever.

But that couldn't be.

"Concentrate."

LAUGH

Robynne jumped, spooked, more scared than she had ever been in her life.

"Concentrate."

A cold tongue licked Robynne's forehead, and she SCREECHED anew. Her foot slipped, and her knee hammered the floor, pain shooting up her leg. She managed to regain her footing, limping, agony shooting through her knee. She looked up.

The door was right ahead of her. How had that happened? She glanced at Rococo, whose face was caked with blood. Rococo looked as if she was running in robotic mode, stepping and pulling, stepping and pulling.

Robynne had to use all her strength to get the door open. She braced it with her foot, and Rococo lugged Marian out of the bedroom. Once out, Robynne felt a sense of relief so total, that her body folded on itself. Her strength left her. She slowly sank to the floor. When she looked back, all she saw was a great darkness, something without a bottom.

She stared, and in the darkness, a figure appeared, a man...perhaps. Then, whatever it was winked out.

That was when Rococo turned and started into the bedroom.

"NO," Robynne said. "No."

Robynne reached out to grab Rococo, but for some reason, Robynne missed. Rococo slipped past, walking slowly back into the darkness, back to Stillwell.

Robynne struggled to her feet. She had to save Rococo. Even as she took a step, the door slammed SHUT.

CHAPTER SEVEN

For a moment, Robynne couldn't think. The closed door kept her from entering the bedroom. Her body ached from the bombardment of the candles. Marian was on the floor, dead to the world. For all Robynne knew, Marian was minutes from death. Yet, Rococo was alone inside the bedroom, which was decidedly horrible. Robynne knew she needed to rescue Rococo, but Robynne also needed to get Marian to safety. There was no safety on the top floor. There was only the deadly bedroom and the urchins. Robynne stood, unable to act. Take Marian to safety or go after Rococo. Robynne was not prepared to choose.

Yet, she had to.

Robynne knew that indecision was the bane of every successful leader. While choosing the wrong path was bad, not choosing was worse. She needed to act, and act swiftly.

She knelt and spoke to Marian.

"I'm taking you to the kitchen," Robynne said. "I'm going to make sure you're safe before I come back for Rococo."

Robynne had no idea if Marian could hear or understand, but that didn't matter.

"You have to help me," Robynne said. "I can't carry you, so you have to take the steps. It's dark, and we don't have a lot of time. We're going to go slow."

Robynne lifted Marian's arm. Then, she did her level best to raise Marian off the floor. The dead weight almost proved too much, but at the last moment, Marian found her feet, helping Robynne, when Robynne needed it most. They stood at the top of the steps, swaying back and forth. Robynne wondered if she dared try the stairs. If they fell… Robynne didn't finish the thought. Falling would probably kill them both.

"Grip the railing," Robynne said. "Use it to steady yourself. We'll do one step at a time. We're in no hurry. Here is the first step."

Robynne stepped down, and for a moment, she thought Marian wouldn't make it. But Marian dragged her feet, zombie style, and moved one step. That was a huge success. If Marian could do one step, she could do them all—or so, Robynne thought.

The journey down the stairs was woefully slow. One step at a time. They had to stop often to regain their strength, and while Robynne wanted to hurry, she knew that hurry was the enemy. Nothing would be worse than seeing Marian lying at the bottom of the steps, her head twisted at an unnatural angle. That was to be avoided at all costs.

Robynne had no idea how long it took to reach the kitchen. Luckily, the lights were still on, so she managed to place Marian in a chair. Then, she found a pint in the fridge and placed it in front of Marian. That Marian didn't grab the pint immediately was testimony to the fog that engulfed Marian. Robynne looked at her phone and was not surprised to find no connection. Stillwell was in charge. That much was obvious.

"There's a pint," Robynne said. "Drink it. I'm going back for Rococo. If you can manage it, check your phone. When you get a chance, call for help. We need more of it than we can let on."

Robynne gently shook Marian's shoulders, but that brought no response either. Robynne grabbed the spare torch from her backpack and headed for the stairs. Her body told her to stop. Her brain told her to stop. Her sense of duty drove her onward. Rococo had volunteered for this, but that didn't mean she needed to suffer the worst. Robynne bit her lip and grabbed the railing. She was going up.

She was going to rescue Rococo.

By the time Robynne reached the last flight of steps, she had come to notice that every flight was steeper than the one before. The last flight resembled a ladder more than stairs. She had to lean into the steps, crawling up and praying that they didn't become totally vertical. She didn't believe she possessed the energy and stamina needed for a vertical climb. Still holding the torch, she climbed on all fours until she reached the top and half tumbled in front of the door to the bedroom.

Panting, she pulled herself erect and turned on her torch. She looked back at the steps and found them as normal as possible. Why had she thought they had turned so steep?

A small voice in the back of her head told her to turn around and go back down. Rococo was, no doubt, already dead. There was no saving her. Robynne would end up like Rococo, another body chucked out the window. If Robynne wanted to save herself, she had to leave. Besides, Marian needed her. Marian, who was lost to the world, needed help, and Robynne was the only one left to help. If Robynne flew out the window, to the joy of the urchins, then Marian was doomed. Didn't Robynne owe Marian a better fate than this? They were friends as well as colleagues.

Robynne pushed the voice out of her brain. She needed to save Rococo, and cowardice wouldn't do.

She grabbed the doorknob, prepared to fight her way into the bedroom. Surprise coursed through her, as the door swung open, as the bedroom welcomed her into the maelstrom.

Even in the dark, Robynne could see Rococo standing still in the middle of the room. Around her whirled four unlit candles, flying about like drones, circling the wiccan who looked oblivious to what was happening. Even as Robynne watched, a candle slammed into Rococo's side, making her flinch, before dropping to the floor, only to zip back into the air. Rococo was the centre of the flying candles and the target of their hate.

Robynne shined the torch on Rococo's bloodied face, and Rococo did not react. She stared ahead, as if mesmerized by something. To Robynne, this was some sort of torture, some kind of medieval punishment. Like being in the stocks, only worse. Outside the urchins chanted. Inside, the candles hammered Rococo with relentless energy.

The urge to lunge ahead and grab Rococo pulsed through Robynne. She ignored the urge. She knew that if she snatched Rococo, the candles would have two targets instead of one. Beyond Rococo, Robynne spotted the open window, the maw that needed to be fed. While the candles were dangerous, the maw was certain death. They had to escape before they became food for the maw.

But how?

Shining the light, Robynne moved toward Rococo. Holding tight to the torch, Robynne slipped close enough to bat a candle out of the air. Then, before it could jump up, Robynne pounced on the candle.

She grabbed it, and the candle came to life in her hand, struggling like some wild animal, trying to get away. Robynne held tight and carried the candle to the maw. As she neared, another candle whammed into her back. She almost turned loose of the candle, but she held on long enough to hurl it into the black hole that was the window. Then, she turned back to the other circling candles.

The next two candles were difficult but not impossible. Robynne managed to snag them with a modicum of effort. That a candle pounded into her head during the chase didn't help Robynne's headache. For a moment, her vision doubled, scaring her, but that passed.

Soon, she faced a single candle that no longer circled Rococo like some moth to a flame. Now, the candle danced about like a firefly, flitting here and there and occasionally taking a beeline for Robynne's face. She managed to duck, but the game was tiring. She had no idea how long she could keep going. All the while, Rococo stood in the middle of the room, blood dripping from her chin.

While Robynne wanted to grab Rococo and leave, Robynne didn't want to try it with the candle circling like some bird of prey. She tried to follow it with the torch, but she wasn't quick enough. The candle darted about, dodging the light.

"Come on, come on, you bloody shit. Come and get me."

But the candle didn't attack. Robynne did the only thing she could think to do. She went to Rococo. She put her arm around the woman and stood close, mindful of the candle.

"I'm going to get you out of here," Robynne said. "But you have to help. You have to do what I say. You have to try."

Robynne had no idea if Rococo even heard. But it didn't matter. The way out was through the door and down the stairs. Anything else was not doable. Keeping a wary eye on the attack candle, Robynne grabbed Rococo's hand.

"Now," Robynne said and tugged at Rococo.

For a moment, Rococo did nothing. A dagger tore at Robynne's heart. If Rococo couldn't move, they were both doomed. The sheer terror inside the room was devastating. It was all Robynne could do to keep from running to a corner, to sob her way to some better place.

"BLOODY HELL!" Robynne yelled. "COME ON!"

This time, the tug started Rococo moving. Not fast, not steady, a stilted gait that lurched rather than walked.

Robynne didn't look at Rococo, as the candle was still flying about, ready to hammer the unready. Robynne still hoped she would be able to knock the candle from the air and rid the room of the hateful things.

They moved at a snail's pace, barely moving for seconds at a time, before covering two steps in a lunge. Robynne panted, her rib screaming with every breath. She needed help. She needed to get out. She should leave the bloodied Rococo behind. That was plain and simple. Staying with Rococo would kill them both.

The candle screamed toward them, and Robynne hit it with the torch, like a cricket bat. The candle skittered across the floor, and for a moment, Robynne considered not going after the candle, but she knew she hadn't "hurt" the candle. Nothing would hurt it. This was her chance to level the playing field, to take away Stillwell's advantage. Robynne let go of Rococo and sped for the candle. She pounced and grabbed the feral thing, holding tight until she was close enough to add the candle to the others already inside the maw. Smiling, feeling self-satisfied, she turned away, only to find Rococo coming toward her, only to find Rococo heading for the window, the certain death that lived inside the darkness.

"NO!" Robynne yelled. "NO!"

Robynne's words did nothing. If anything, they caused Rococo to speed up, hurtling toward her like some runaway train. Robynne braced for the impact, and when Rococo hit, agony blasted through Robynne's body. Her breath disappeared. She couldn't move. Despite her best efforts, Rococo drove them both toward the window, toward death.

Robynne was certain she didn't have the strength to resist Rococo. In another time or place, Robynne would have been just fine, but this was not another time or place. Rococo was some sort of juggernaut, pushing Robynne back. There was a relentless quality to the battle. Rococo was summoned by the window, and Rococo was going to make it—Robynne be damned.

LAUGH.

That was when Robynne gave up trying to stop Rococo. Robynne did the only thing she could think to do. She dropped to the floor and tackled Rococo. It was the most painful thing she had ever done, but she brought Rococo down. That allowed Robynne to jump on top of Rococo, pinning her in front of the window.

At first, Rococo bucked, trying to get loose, but like Robynne, Rococo had run out of energy. She was still beneath Robynne, who leaned close to whisper into Rococo's ear.

"If you keep fighting me, we will both die. Do you hear me? We will both die."

For a moment, Rococo did nothing. Then, she spoke.

"Die."

CHAPTER EIGHT

Robynne shivered, but she didn't move. She didn't know if Rococo wanted to die or wanted Robynne to die. Could that be possible? Robynne didn't want to make a mistake. Stillwell was enemy enough. Stillwell and Rococo would be fatal.

"Rococo," Robynne said, "Rococo, are you...aware? Do you know who I am?"

Rococo didn't answer, which sent a chill through Robynne. What the bloody hell was Rococo up to?

"ROCOCO!" Robynne yelled over the whine and wind and chanting. "LISTEN TO ME! WE HAVE TO GET OUT OF HERE! WE HAVE TO GO NOW! OTHERWISE, WE WON'T LEAVE AT ALL. DO YOU HEAR ME?!"

Robynne thought she saw Rococo nod. It wasn't clear, it wasn't definite, but it seemed to be a nod. That was enough for Robynne. She rolled off Rococo and stayed on hands and knees. Even as she did, everything stopped.

The whine vanished.

The chanting stopped.

Robynne glanced over her shoulder, expecting the maw to be gone.

It wasn't.

The gaping hole was still there, pulsing, almost whispering. It was like some hungry animal, waiting for another person to feed it. Robynne stared, unable to turn away. The thing was terrible, freakish and demanding. It seemed to smile at her, and she SCREAMED. It was the worst thing she had ever seen. She felt her mind begin to slip. She was imagining the maw, the hunger, the danger.

"It's just a window," Robynne said. "Just a window. Don't look. It's just a window. Don't...look. It's just...just a...window."

Robynne felt Rococo's hand on her shoulder. Robynne felt Rococo's hot breath.

"Come," Rococo said. "Come."

Robynne felt her head being turned. She wasn't doing it. Someone else was forcing her eyes away from the window, the maw, the thing that needed more. Even as her face moved, she wanted to look back, to gaze upon the dark. She couldn't leave it. It was hungry.

Rococo's face filled Robynne's vision. They were nose to nose.

As they touched, Robynne felt a spear of heat run through her. She needed to move, to go, before the cold found her again, before the maw could tantalize her, woo her.

"We have to get out," Robynne said.

"Yes," Rococo said.

They grabbed hands and stood. Robynne's torch still worked, and she flashed it around the room. She felt strange, out of sorts, as if the room was wrong somehow. What was it?

"Come on," Rococo said. "Before—"

The lens of Robynne's torch exploded in a cloud of plastic fragments. For a moment, the light refracted in all directions and colours, like being inside a rainbow, or some kind of colour cascade. It was ethereal, mesmerizing, a swarm of colour flies, fluttering about in random disorder. It was beautiful, for an instant, a long instant.

The bulb in the torch exploded, and the light disappeared.

Rococo screamed.

"LET ME GO!" Rococo yelled. "LET ME GO!"

Robynne reached out, grasping as Rococo was dragged past. Their fingers touched for a moment, but Robynne couldn't hold on. In the dark, Robynne was sure of nothing, except someone was pulling Rococo to the window. That was clear. Robynne turned, and the chanting overwhelmed her. The voices echoed through the room, making Robynne recoil.

The voices hammered her, drowning out Rococo's screams. Yet, she had to go after Rococo.

Robynne lunged, her hands in front, feeling for Rococo. Her hands found a wall of icy air, that made her fingertips tingle. She pushed through the wall, the cold ripping the air from her lungs. The need for speed drove her. The maw waited. The chanting grew faster. No part of her wanted to keep going, but she couldn't stop. She lunged and tripped over something. She crashed, and pain filled her chest. Even in the dark, she knew she had tripped over Rococo. Gasping, she spun toward the body. In a moment, Robynne had wrapped her arms around Rococo's legs. Robynne stopped the progress of the body.

Eyes closed tight against the pain, Robynne held on. She knew she couldn't last long. She didn't have the strength. Stillwell was stopped for the moment, but he wasn't beaten. The window yearned for them. Stillwell wanted victims, perhaps ghosts to join him in the hell of the bedroom.

A cold tongue licked Robynne's cheek. She SCREAMED, twisting away her head. But the licking persisted, worse than ever, like a dog, but without any warmth. Long, stinging swaths covered her face, even though she wagged her head back and forth. The feeling was eerie, maddening. Her heart jumped into her throat, as the frigid tongue probed her ear.

"NOOOOOOOOO!"

Robynne's denial chased off the tongue for a moment. She swallowed hard and crawled toward Rococo's head. Robynne's fingers found Rococo's cheek, a cheek inhumanly cold.

"Oh god," Robynne said. "Oh, god. Rococo! Rococo!"

Rococo moaned, and Robynne felt a hint of possibility, a chance.

"We're going to crawl," Robynne said. "We're going to crawl out of here. We're going to do it hand-in-hand. Don't. Let. Go."

Robynne had never felt so tired and in pain. She needed to rest. She needed to sleep. She needed whiskey. She needed to escape bloody Stillwell and his damned window.

Robynne held onto Rococo's hand. They moved away from the window.. Robynne was sure of that. The evil of the maw was like a chain attached to their legs. They had to keep that...thing, at their backs. They had to move away from the chanting. The direction wasn't difficult. The door was ahead of them. Robynne forced herself to focus on the door. Salvation was outside the door. Safety was on the other side. They just had to make it out, out to the other side.

"R...r...obynne," Rococo said.

"Don't try to talk," Robynne said. "Keep moving."

"I...c...ant."

"You have to."

"L...ea...ve me."

"No," Robynne said. "It's just a few more feet. We can make it."

"Too....tired."

"Don't talk. Crawl!"

Rococo collapsed to the floor, and for a moment, Robynne thought the wiccan had died.

"Rococo, Rococo," Robynne said. "Get up. For god's sake, get up."

"C....old." Rococo said.

"You're not cold." Robynne snuggled up to Rococo. "You're not cold. You need to move, that will warm you." Robynne wrapped her arms around the wiccan. "We're going to pause for a moment. We're going to get warm. But we can't stay, Rococo. We have to move. To stay is to die."

"Die."

"No, not die. Live. We're going to live. Do you understand? We're going to get out of this bloody bedroom, and we're going to live."

"Die," Rococo repeated.

"Live." Robynne leaned very close, her lips to Rococo's ear. "You're going to get your bloody, lazy arse moving. I'm sick and tired of your lollygagging."

Robynne pulled back and yelled. "Do you understand? You're going to get your body moving. Do you hear me? You're coming with me. No more lagging behind, wiccan. Chant some energy spell and get on your hands and knees. We're getting out of here. We're going to pick up Marian and get out of this bloody house. And after we rest for a day or two, we're coming back and getting rid of Stillwell once and for all. So, saddle up, witch. We don't have time for a nap. Get up!"

Robynne slapped Rococo's arse.

"UP!"

Rococo rose, and Robynne grabbed the wiccan's hand. Together they started for the door, even as a wave of hate swept over them. It felt as if some giant hand was trying to squash them. With the hand came a hopeless feeling, something that told Robynne she would never make it, never escape. She could continue to resist, but her energy would be wasted. She couldn't get out. She would be meat for the maw. A kind of ennui attacked her muscles. If she couldn't win, why play?

Robynne leaned over and bit her own arm. The pain felt clean somehow. She bit harder, drawing blood. Her blood was warm and tasted of salt and copper, and while it bothered her to draw her own blood, it also reassured her.

She was still alive. And she was going to stay alive.

Rococo showed real strength, making Robynne feel hopeful. Blood seeped from the bite, and that too helped. They were going to make it.

Then, the first shard hit her hand.

The sting was immediate, making Robynne wonder if some bone or ligament had snapped. That was all she needed, a balky hand. She was tempted to stop and check out her hand, but that was absolutely the wrong thing to do. She had to keep moving.

Then, something raked across her forehead.

The sting was unmistakable. Robynne heard Rococo yelp, and Robynne knew a new torture had begun. Her other hand was stung, as if by some bee. Her neck was stung. What sort of insect was after them?

No insect.

Robynne knew that the "insects" were nothing more than the plastic pieces from the torch lens. They were whipped by some unseen force, flying about, slicing across her skin. They didn't cut, not deep, but she knew they left scratches, perhaps bloody scratches. They wouldn't kill, but that wasn't their job. Their job was to keep Rococo and Robynne in the room.

"Keep going!" Robynne insisted. "We can't stop."

The infernal snips of plastic attacked any uncovered skin. Hands, neck, face, Robynne wondered how they managed to avoid her eyes, even as one cut through her eyelash.

Bloody hell.

Stillwell was trying to blind her. Had no idea what to do. In the dark, she couldn't see the swarm of plastic.

In the dark.

If she was going to stay in the dark, then she didn't need her eyes. She leaned closer to Rococo.

"Pull your shirt over your face," Robynne said.

"Huh?"

"To keep them from cutting your eyes. Pull up your shirt."

Robynne took a moment, to pull her shirt over her face, even as a shard hit the fabric. Her shirt wasn't much, but it was enough. She could feel Rococo pulling up her shirt, and then, truly blind, they pushed on. Robynne knew they weren't far from the door. She felt the hungry maw behind.

"Now," Robynne said. "Now."

For some seconds, the shards continued to attack Robynne's face. While Robynne felt some pressure, she felt no stings. The shirt was working. She wanted to thumb her nose at Stillwell, but she didn't have time or energy. Her victory was short-lived. A shard skipped across her abdomen, leaving a long sting that made her gasp.

The gasp sent a shock of pain through her chest. Then, like a cloud of angry hornets, the plastic attacked her bare flesh.

There was a moment, when she thought to pull down her shirt, but that would make her face vulnerable.

That was a bad trade. Instead, she steeled herself against the swarm, making herself move and trying to keep from breathing too deeply. Then, when she thought she couldn't continue, her head hit something.

The wall.

Rococo moaned, and Robynne gasped. There was a moment of indecision. Which direction should they take? Where was the door. She felt the unbridled hate from behind, so, she couldn't go that way.

But left, or right?

A mistake would cost her, as her energy was flagging. The angry shards were having an effect. She felt to one side, seeking something that would indicate a door.

"Rococo," Robynne said. "Reach out, find the door."

After some seconds, Robynne knew the door had not been found. She also knew they couldn't be still.

The combined chanting and shards and hate were too much. She was more than a little afraid that they both were going to die.

"Grab my ankle," Robynne told Rococo. "And don't let go. We'll go slow, but we have to keep going. I'm going to turn."

Robynne turned, and she felt Rococo grab on. That was a good sign. Then, Robynne commenced the slow crawl, keeping the wall to her left, feeling along the floor. If she had guessed right, they would soon find the door. If not, they would crawl about the room...to the maw, to the power that would suck them from the room.

The shards didn't stop. One zipped across her cheek, and Robynne felt a sting.

What?

She took a moment to feel the shirt over her face, and, in horror, she discovered that it had been cut through in many places. It was taking the slashes meant for her face. Tears fell from her eyes, as the certainty of her death loomed. Why was she even trying? She should lie down and let Stillwell have his way.

Then, her fingers found the door jamb. Hope surged through Robynne, as she reached up to find the doorknob. In seconds, she had gripped and twisted. The door was reluctant, but Robynne managed to butt it open with her shoulder. As it swung wide, she crawled out of the bedroom. Rococo followed, still holding onto Robynne's ankle.

They both cleared the doorway, even as the door closed on its own. Robynne shivered from head to toe. They had escaped. They had made it.

Then, as if all air had left the balloon, Robynne collapsed.

"Oh, no." Rococo said.

Right before Robynne fainted.

CHAPTER NINE

Robynne woke in the dark. For a long moment, she wondered where she was. Was she home? No, her bed was softer than what she was lying on. So, she wasn't in her room, dreaming. She was...in the house, Stillwell's house. If she remembered correctly, she was outside the master bedroom, the one haunted by Stillwell, owned by Stillwell, desecrated by Stillwell. But she wasn't alone. Rococo was there with her, next to her—somewhere.

Robynne reached out, searching for Rococo. Robynne's hand waved back and forth, but she felt nothing. Rococo should have been within reach. Where was she? Robynne took a deep breath, and pain seared her lungs. The agony reminded her that she had broken a rib. How could she forget that? She rolled to her knees. Her body hurt in a dozen places, reminding her that she had been pummelled by candles.

The candles reminded her of the other flying objects. She touched her hands and arms, her face. Her fingers made her skin burn. She recalled the plastic shards. She was one mass of sores and pain.

"Rococo," Robynne whispered. "Rococo."

No answer.

Robynne realized she was alone. Rococo was not close by. Wait, where was Marian. Robynne had come with Marian and Rococo. Marian was...in the kitchen. Robynne remembered. Marian had had...troubles. She was resting. Marian was resting.

Where was Rococo"?

Robynne pushed herself to her feet. She felt her way until she reached the stairs. Then, she started down, carefully holding onto the railing. She moved slowly. While she didn't expect Stillwell to attack, she wasn't about to take chances.

The lights were on in the kitchen, and for a moment, Robynne wanted to cry. She had been in the dark so long. The light was so welcome. She looked about. Marian sat at the table, her head down, asleep—or dead.

Robynne gasped. How had that idea popped into her head? She limped across the room and stood by Marian. For a moment, Robynne was afraid to touch.

"Marian," Robynne whispered. "Marian."

Marian moaned, and Robynne let out a sigh.

"Oh, bloody hell," Robynne said and hugged Marian.

"Robynne?" Marian asked and raised her head. "Robynne?"

They hugged. Robynne had the feeling she was safe, safe at last.

"I'll make tea," Robynne said.

"We have to find Rococo."

"We will, but after tea—and some pain pills."

"That makes sense. How rotten do you feel?"

"Like a worn boot, beat up everywhere."

"Me too. I suppose Rococo feels the same."

They lapsed into silence as Robynne fixed tea and found the pain pills. As they sipped, they joined hands, as if holding onto one another would somehow ease the pain.

"What happened to your face and arms?" Marian asked.

"The torch lens broke."

"Must have been a bloody big explosion."

"No, just chaff Stillwell could use against us."

Marian frowned, and Robynne explained how the lens debris had become a swarm of cutting insects.

"That's horrible," Marian said.

"It's Stillwell."

"After we find her, do we go back up?" Marian asked.

"Not tonight. We've run out of torches, and well, I think we will do better in daylight."

"So, we are going to try."

"I think we owe ourselves one more go."

"And if Rococo doesn't want to?"

"Well, the marriage thing didn't work so well, did it?"

"Worth a try. So, what is the plan this time?"

"We close the window."

"How do you propose to do that?"

"I'm not sure, but that's where we start."

Marian nodded. "Ready to go hunt?"

"A few more minutes."

"Exactly."

At that moment, Rococo staggered into the room. Robynne stood and guided Rococo to the table.

"Cuppa?" Robynne asked.

Rococo nodded.

"We're going back," Marian said, as Robynne went to get tea. "In the morning."

"Dawn's not far off."

"You don't have to go with us," Marian said.

"But I do," Rococo said. "I owe it to you and...him."

"You don't owe him anything," Robynne said.

Rococo offered a wan smile. "You know, Stillwell is the first ghost I've ever really met. I mean, there have been knocks and moans and clattering in the night, but Stillwell is there. He's proof."

"Proof?" Marian asked.

"That ghosts exist, that a person can become a ghost."

Robynne returned with the tea. "You doubted before?"

"Who doesn't?"

Robynne held out her hands. Marian took one, Rococo the other.

"We're going up there with the sun. And we're going to shut the window."

"Yes," Marian said.

"Yes," Rococo said.

Robynne smiled. "Now, let's sleep."

The morning arrived grey and dreary. Over morning tea, Robynne considered their bravery of the night before. Did they really want to test Stillwell again? They had lost twice now. Was the third try the charm? She had her doubts, so she put it to the others.

"I know what we said before, but we can walk, if we want."

"I will go with the decision." Marian said.

"I'm game," Rococo replied. "I think I owe it to myself to correct my mistakes."

"Enough said," Robynne finished. "Finish your tea. Let's go get that son of a bitch."

Standing outside the bedroom door, Robynne recalled the horror of the dark, the terror of the room. She knew what to expect. The chanting, the wind, the chaff...the window. The window was the goal. They needed to close the maw.

"Straight to the window," Robynne said. "We close it and deny Stillwell its power."

"I will distract him," Rococo said. "You two close it."

"All right. Ready?"

"No," Marian sort of whimpered, "But that makes no difference."

"Ready then?" Rococo asked.

The door opened easily, an invitation to enter. Robynne shivered, even as she forced herself through the doorway.

Even though the window stood open, no light came through. The other windows, the draped windows gave the room a half-light, but the maw was as black as ever. Robynne hesitated, as nothing was moving in the room at the moment. She was certain that would soon change.

"Stillwell," Rococo said as she stepped into the middle of the room. "You have had enough fun with us. I am here to marry you and take you to a warm place. Come, let us make history. You shall have a loving wife."

A ghastly grey light appeared in one corner, a spectre that looked ill and tainted. Robynne bit her lip to keep from screaming. Rococo turned to the thing.

"There you are. Don't you tire of this game? Come, join me." Rococo held out her hand.

The spectre seemed to move, taking a half step. Robynne waited. The calm was as eerie as the swarm of plastic. Robynne wondered if the gesture would be enough. It seemed to be working. She stared, gauging the movement in the scant light. Was it enough?

Then, Marian broke for the window.

In an instant, the spectre disappeared. A blast of cold air batted them. Marian was hurled backwards, away from the window. She crashed into the far wall and dropped to the floor, unmoving. Robynne hesitated, not knowing what to do. As she waited, the plastic chaff rose off the floor and began to whirl about, spinning and bobbing in the greyness. Robynne stared, afraid to move, lest the horde come after her. Rococo smiled, the centre of the angry things.

"Do not mind her," Rococo said. "This is between us, Stillwell. We must create our pact and seize our destiny. You know what is best. You know how to end your hate."

Chanting filled the room.

Robynne started for the window, but she didn't run. She didn't want to draw attention to herself. She edged, a little at a time, as Rococo continued to talk to the ghost, as the chaff spun around, as Marian lay in a heap by the far wall, as the maw pulsated black and ominous.

Keeping her eyes on Rococo and the chaff, Robynne took baby steps, like a child sneaking up on a biscuit jar. If Stillwell stayed distracted, Robynne might have a chance to pull the drapes, to cut off the chanting. She didn't dare turn away. There was too much at stake.

"Think," Rococo said. "Consider what your life will be like when you leave this place, when you come with me. Your dreams will come true. The thing you want most you will have. Think, Stillwell, don't you wish to abandon this dreary life? Don't you wish for something better?"

Robynne must have moved too quickly, because with the suddenness of a bee swarm, the plastic chards whipped across the room, right for her. She threw up her arms to protect her face, but it was little good against the creatures and their sharp edges. She batted them from the air, but they remained on the floor but a second before they took to the air again and joined the mob. She backed toward a wall, hoping to protect her back. If she could do that, she could tiptoe her way along the wall until she found the window.

While Robynne could hear Rococo, Robynne was far too busy to watch. She had the idea that Rococo was immune somehow, not plagued by the gnats of plastic. It was all Robynne could do to keep from being blinded. She had slowed to a snail's pace, but she forced herself to keep moving, despite the torture of a thousand scratches.

"OVER HERE!"

Robynne peeked between fingers. Across the room, Marian stood by the wall.

"OVER HERE!" Marian yelled a second time.

The swarm turned and zipped toward Marian. Robynne took the opportunity to move faster, to get the window, to pull the drapes. The urchins' chant blasted inside her head, but she moved, keeping an eye on Marian and the swarm. Robynne reached the window and grabbed the drape.

She looked up in time to see Rococo being pulled toward the window. Robynne looked up in time to see the plastic mob coming at her. The attack was furious. Rococo was heading for the maw. Marian had gone silent. Robynne hoped she was all right. As Robynne started to pull the drape across the maw, icy fingers seized her wrist.

Robynne SCREAMED.

And let go of the drape.

There was a moment of shear panic, as Robynne shook her hand and arm in an attempt to rid herself of the fingers of death. She forgot about Marian and Rococo. Robynne could think of nothing but escaping from the frigid clutch. She used her good hand to knock the fingers from her wrist, but the cold lingered.

"ROBIN?!"

Robynne turned to the voice, to Rococo, who was losing her fight to stay out of the window, the black maw. Robynne saw Rococo leaning away from the window, like a mountain climber going up a steep grade. Despite Rococo's effort, she was being sucked back inch by inch.

Robynne lunged from the window and grabbed Rococo's arm. Immediately, Robynne planted her feet and tried to take Rococo away. For a moment, they made some progress, but then they came to a full stop. They were locked in place by some sort of gravity, something that would take them to their deaths.

"Grab my belt," Robynne told Rococo. "We'll do this in tandem."

Robynne felt Rococo grab hold of Robynne's belt, which allowed Robynne to use her arms to generate more energy. She leaned away from the window and pushed with all she had.

She felt like some kind of weightlifter trying to pull a bus or something. She knew Rococo was trying too, and for some seconds, they moved a foot or two. But the void—the maw possessed a pull they could not match. Robynne SCREAMED, but it did little good.

"I'll do it," Rococo said.

"What?" Robynne asked.

Robynne received no answer, as Rococo let go of Robynne's belt. Robynne fell on her face, barely catching herself. Then, she rolled over.

Rococo was drawn into the maw, and Rococo made no effort to get away. There was a smile on Rococo's face, some sort of peace. Robynne could do nothing but stare, as Rococo was sucked through the window and into the abyss.

The chanting stopped.

The spinning chaff dropped to the floor.

Sunlight poured through the window that had been the maw.

Robynne felt no pull, no hate.

She slowly stood and walked to the window. She sank to her knees and peeked over the sill.

On the sidewalk below was the battered, dead Rococo, blood all about her head.

That was when Robynne began to cry, to sob. Huge gasps and spasms rocked her. She closed her eyes, as if not looking would somehow make things different. But they weren't different.

Rococo was dead.

That certainty burned Robynne's brain.

Rococo was dead.

A huge anger flared inside Robynne. A heated ire consumed her insides. She was not going to take this. She was not going to allow it to happen.

"STILLWELL!" Robynne screamed. "STILLWELL! YOU ARE GOING TO LEAVE, AND YOU ARE GOING TO LEAVE THIS INSTANT. DO YOU UNDERSTAND?"

Robynne waited, looking about the room.

Laugh.

The snarky laugh came from the corner, and Robynne turned to it.

Foolish girl. You are next.

A grey spectre appeared in the corner. Stillwell, in his evil grey, grinned at her. Robynne began to shake, as the hot anger cooled. She felt a pull at her back, a tug, and she knew the maw had returned. The blackness was behind her. She took a step. The chanting resumed. The truce was over. Chaff leaped off the floor and spun in all directions.

Robynne knew what that meant. She pulled against the tug, even as she knew she was not strong enough to get loose.

But she was not going to give up. She wouldn't make it easy.

Stillwell!

Robynne knew the voice and knew it wasn't possible. Rococo was dead, lying in blood on the sidewalk. Robynne turned, and there was Rococo. No, not Rococo, but the spectre of Rococo, and she was not as grey as Stillwell. She was more white, brighter, and she moved with a grace Robynne admired.

Stay away.

It is time, Stillwell.

After I do her.

Now, Stillwell.

Robynne watched, and for a moment the spectres seemed to mingle, becoming one in some fashion. Then, they flew together, straight past Robynne and into the maw.

Nothing happened.

Then, the maw imploded, sucking all the darkness into a single mote that winked out.

The chaff fell from the air.

The chanting faded to nothing.

The window, the sunlit window was all there was.

Robynne rubbed her chilled wrist and stared, waiting for Stillwell to reappear.

Nothing happened.

A great weariness descended upon Robynne. She rubbed her chest where the pain originated. She touched the scratches on her skin. She was tired, terribly tired. She shuffled slowly to Marian.

"Marian," Robynne said.

Marian's eyes opened. "Are we dead yet?" Marian asked.

"Not yet," Robynne answered.

"Rococo?"

"She went out the window and saved us."

Marian frowned.

"I'll explain later. Come, let's close the window. I think it will let us."

Together, Robynne and Marian closed the window, but they did not close the drapes. The sunlight felt too good. Then, they limped for the stairs.

"What...what will we tell them?" Marian asked.

"That she lost her balance and fell out. Nothing more."

"He's gone?"

"He's gone."

EPILOGUE

James stood to one side, watching the bricklayers ply their trade. "Are you sure this is needed?" he asked.

Robynne and Marian stood next to James. The women had come back for the sealing of the window. While they had overcome the shock of their night in the room, neither wanted to try another night.

"No, we're not sure it's needed," Marian said. "But it feels absolutely right. I mean, leaving this window unbricked would be an invitation."

"Let's just call it an overabundance of caution," Robynne said. "And, in fact, you don't need the window. There are several others that let in adequate light."

"It seems sacrilegious in some sense," James was almost puzzled. "I'm changing the house in order to keep out a ghost?"

"Don't think of it that way," Robynne said. "Think of it as a way to keep anyone from pitching out."

"Oh, right," James nodded disbelievingly, "Like that woman you had with you?"

"Rococo had a misadventure," Marian said. "In the dark, things can happen."

"Couldn't I just keep the window locked?"

"You could," Robynne said. "But locks can be unlocked, and closed windows can open. Do I think that will happen now? No, I am convinced that we rid this place of its ghost. But no one is privy to the wherewithal of ghosts. This window seems particularly vulnerable."

"Hang a tapestry over it, and you'll never know what used to be here," Marian offered.

James laughed at that. "All right. Well then, if you two are satisfied, then I am also." He paused and nodded. "I don't know if this would be a good time, but I have a friend, well, actually a business colleague, who bought an old nunnery in the north. She swears there are some very odd things happening inside the Abbey."

"Ghostly things?" Robynne asked.

"Very ghostly, according to her. Anyway, I was wondering if I might pass along your names. Would you be up for a bit more ghost hunting?"

Robynne looked at Marian who smiled.

"We would be happy to meet her acquaintance," Marian said.

"But that doesn't mean we'll take the job," Robynne said.

"Of course not," James said. "I'll let her know that she can contact you and discuss the project."

"Tell her we will need a detailed history of the monastery, if she can find one," Robynne said.

"And a list of wiccans in the area," Marian added.

"Wiccans?"

"We have found that they can be immensely helpful, under the right circumstances."

"I'll pass along your requirements. Anything else?"

"That should be enough," Robynne said.

Robynne and Marian didn't stay for the entire bricking of the window. Instead, they drifted to the nearest pub and found a handy booth. Their pints arrived before they discussed the offer James had alluded to.

"Well, what do you think?" Robynne asked, letting the ale warm her a little.

"I don't know," Marian said. "I have this awful feeling that we're going to go into that nunnery and be inundated by Gregorian chants."

Robynne laughed. "I imagine they would sound better than a flock of street kids."

"True, but there might be more than one ghost to deal with. That would complicate matters, wouldn't it?"

"We don't have to take the job."

"If we do take it, I want a gobsmack amount of money."

"That goes without saying."

Robynne held up her pint. "We should do this. To Rococo, may she and Stillwell rest in peace."

"Hear, hear."

They clicked glasses and sipped.

THE END

I hope that you enjoyed this book.

If you are willing to leave a short and honest review for me on Amazon, it will be very much appreciated, as reviews help to get my books noticed.

Over the page you will find a preview of one the Ghost Hunters Book One

PREVIEW The Haunting of Forsaken Manor

THE BRITISH HAUNTINGS SERIES

CAT KNIGHT

THE
HAUNTING
OF
FORSAKEN MANOR
GHOST HUNTERS BOOK ONE

PROLOGUE

Stillwell pulled back the curtain and looked down into the street. From his fourth-floor vantage point, he could see the children across the street, the urchins that gathered most mornings, ragamuffins that should have been working in his estimation. They were shabby and dirty, the worst of the ones that avoided their homes and the parents that beat them. Stillwell knew them. He knew them well, since they hectored him like a nagging wife.

Nagging wife.

What did Stillwell know about a nagging wife? What did he know about any wife? What did he know about anything?

He stared at the urchins, even as several more joined the passel on the sidewalk. He recognized most of them. They were regulars. They smiled at each other and cuffed each other like school pals. He hated them. He hated their easy camaraderie, their smiles. They had nothing, nothing at all, and they acted as if they owned the world. It was bonkers, to his way of thinking. They should have been miserable—like him.

The cough came from deep in his lungs, down to his gut. Did his lungs extend to his gut? Were they that big? No, no, he remembered enough anatomy from school to realize the racking cough couldn't start that low.

He bent over in pain, coughing, coughing, grabbing a handkerchief to catch the bloody phlegm that came with the cough. It was getting worse, much worse, but he no longer cared. He cared for nothing, especially not the urchins and their mock.

Somewhat recovered, Stillwell went back to the window. He peeked. The urchin mob across the street had grown. There were a number of new faces that he didn't recognize. Did every snot-drivel in London want to serenade him? Where were the Bobbies? Where were the urchins' parents? Oh, Stillwell knew where the parents were. They were passed out from the ale they had consumed the night before. The parents wanted nothing to do with the wastrels that raced through the streets, causing mayhem and avoiding the police. Stillwell knew, and he hated it.

Another coughing session sent Stillwell to his knees. Was he feverish? He felt his forehead, and he swore he was feverish.

When had he last eaten?

He couldn't remember.

He left the window for a moment and limped to the table by his bed. The whiskey was on the table, and it was the only thing that seemed to quell the coughing. He poured a generous dollop and threw it down, feeling the heat in his belly. For the moment, the pain and the coughs were squelched.

When had he last eaten?

He couldn't remember.

The knock at the door made him frown.

"What do you want?" he called out.

"Mr. Caine," the woman said. "Are you all right?"

Stillwell recognized the voice. It was the maid, Martha, the woman who hounded him from morning till night. Was he all right? Did he need something? Did he want something to eat? Bah! He knew her and hated her, almost as much as he hated the urchins across the street. Stillwell had come to hate everyone.

Everyone?

Yes, when he thought about it, he hated everyone, just as he hated leaving his home, which he never did, or his room, which he seldom did. He was filled with hatred from morning till night till morning. He lived on hate, thrived on it. If he had his way, the urchins on the sidewalk would be consigned to whaling ships as cabin boys. They would be gone for years at a time, at the mercy of rough sailors who would just as soon throw the cabin boy over the railing as to take any guff. Stillwell would do the same with the girls too. A few years at sea would teach them a bit of discipline and the proper way to address one's betters.

"I'm quite well," Stillwell said to the door. "Now, please go."

He heard Martha descend the stairs. From his fourth-floor bedroom, he had a commanding view of the street, of the urchins. A cannon would do nicely for the mob. One load of grapeshot would reduce their numbers considerably. He smiled at the thought. A bit of blood and gore was exactly what the other children needed. It would teach them how to act, how to restrain themselves. In fact, he would be doing the world a favour, if he reduced the number of untamed vermin on the streets. They might just give him a medal.

Stillwell smiled at that. A medal would show everyone that he wasn't the monster the urchins supposed. He was human too.

At the sound of the voices, he turned from the door. He almost ran to the window, unmindful of the pain in his chest, the agony in his hip.

Damn those urchins, damn them to hell.

He peeked past the curtain. He saw the urchins. He heard them chant.

Stillwell went to wed
On a lovely summer day.
He stood alone at the altar
Till the pastor went away.
Why was he the last to know
That she had found another beau?

Stillwell hated the chant, hated it to the depths of his being. Every morning, they chanted. Every morning, his hatred grew. Every morning, he cursed her and everyone else he had ever known, everyone he would ever meet.

Having had enough, Stillwell pulled aside the curtains and opened the window.

"BEGONE!" he shouted. "BEGONE, OR I WILL CURSE YOU AND YOURS FOR ALL ETERNITY! DO YE HEAR ME, YOU LITTLE MONSTERS?! BEGONE!"

The children stopped chanting.

Stillwell smiled. The tiny bastards could be silenced by a man of some consequence—and a threat.

But it wasn't a threat, as far as Stillwell was concerned. He hated the urchins, and if they didn't flee, he would call upon the devils of Hades to come and rain fire and brimstone on the ill-clad and ill-fed lot.

"DO YE HEAR ME?!" he shouted afresh. "BEGONE BEFORE I SEND YOUR SOULS TO SATAN HIMSELF!"

But they didn't run.

They didn't cry.

They laughed, the laugh of the doomed.

Stillwell went to wed

On a lovely summer day.

He stood alone at the altar

Till the pastor went away.

Why was he the last to know

That she had found another beau?

The chant infuriated Stillwell, and he leaned out farther, shaking his fist, almost screaming.

Until the cough began.

It was the cough from his innards, from that place where his strength resided. It bubbled up his chest and squeezed his lungs. He felt his heart rattle inside his chest. It was the cough of a dying man.

Stillwell held onto the window frame for as long as he could. But as the coughing continued, his vision faded, turning to black, robbing him of his sight, his strength. His fingers failed. He tumbled out the window.

The urchins watched, some not quite understanding what was happening. Stillwell hit the sidewalk, and the blood spattered. It was only then that the children slowly stopped chanting.

Why was he the last to know

That she found another... beau?

READ THE REST

HERE ARE SOME OF MY OTHER BOOKS

Ghosts and Haunted Houses: a British Hauntings Collection

Sixteen books– http://a-fwd.to/58aWoW8

The British Hauntings Series

The Haunting of Elleric Lodge - http://a-fwd.to/6aa9u0N

The Haunting of Fairview House - http://a-fwd.to/6lKwbG1

The Haunting of Weaver House - http://a-fwd.to/7Do5KDi

The Haunting of Grayson House - http://a-fwd.to/3nu8fqk

The Haunting of Keira O'Connell - http://a-fwd.to/2qrTERv

The Haunting of Ferncoombe Manor http://a-fwd.to/32MzXfz

The Haunting of Highcliff Hall - http://a-fwd.to/2Fsd7F6

The Haunting of Harrow House - http://a-fwd.to/aQkzLPf

The Haunting of Stone Street Cemetery http://a-fwd.to/1txL6vk

The Haunting of Rochford House http://a-fwd.to/6hbXYp0

The Haunting of Knoll House http://a-fwd.to/1GC9MrD

The Haunting of the Grey Lady http://a-fwd.to/4EUSjb7

The Haunting of Blakely Manor http://a-fwd.to/3b2B631

The Yuletide Haunting http://a-fwd.to/7a5QF4S

The Haunting of Fort Recluse http://a-fwd.to/3Hz77IX

The Haunting Trap http://a-fwd.to/5hw7zJ8

The Haunting of Montgomery House http://a-fwd.to/20ia6sP

The Haunting of Mackenzie Keep http://a-fwd.to/7n2AWxp

The Haunting of Gatesworld Manor http://a-fwd.to/3XlZUEK

The Haunting of The Lost Traveller Tavern http://a-fwd.to/3GAG1nG

The Haunting of the House on the Hill http://a-fwd.to/1X2Wtcn

The Haunting of Hemlock Grove Manor http://a-fwd.to/LpE0k9j

The Ghost Sight Chronicles

The Haunting on the Ridgeway - http://a-fwd.to/1bGBJ6O

Cursed to Haunt - http://a-fwd.to/7BiHzLj

The Revenge Haunting. http://a-fwd.to/67V0NBO

About the Author

Cat Knight has been fascinated by fantasy and the paranormal since she was a child. Where others saw animals in clouds, Cat saw giants and spirits. A mossy rock was home to faeries, and laying beneath the earth another dimension existed.

That was during the day.

By night there were evil spirits lurking in the closet and under her bed. They whirled around her in the witching hour, daring her to come out from under her blanket and face them. She breathed in a whisper and never poked her head out from under her covers nor got up in the dark no matter how scared she was, because for sure, she would die at the hands of ghosts or demons.

How she ever grew up without suffocating remains a mystery.

RECEIVE THE

HAUNTING OF LILAC

HOUSE FREE!

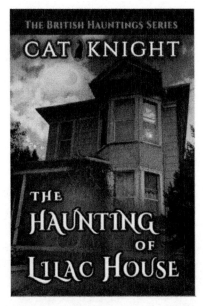

When you subscribe to Cat Knight's newsletter for new release announcements

SUBSCRIBE HERE

Like me on Facebook

Printed in Great Britain
by Amazon